W9-CTT-532

SPEED RACER

Born to Race

Adapted by Michael Anthony Steele

Based upon the film *Speed Racer* written by The Wachowski Brothers.

PSS!
PRICE STERN SLOAN

PRICE STERN SLOAN
Published by the Penguin Group
Penguin Group (USA) Inc., 375 Hudson Street, New York, New York 10014, USA
Penguin Group (Canada), 90 Eglinton Avenue East, Suite 700,
Toronto, Ontario M4P 2Y3, Canada
(a division of Pearson Penguin Canada Inc.)
Penguin Books Ltd., 80 Strand, London WC2R 0RL, England
Penguin Group Ireland, 25 St. Stephen's Green, Dublin 2, Ireland
(a division of Penguin Books Ltd.)
Penguin Group (Australia), 250 Camberwell Road, Camberwell, Victoria 3124, Australia
(a division of Pearson Australia Group Pty. Ltd.)
Penguin Books India Pvt. Ltd., 11 Community Centre, Panchsheel Park,
New Delhi—110 017, India
Penguin Group (NZ), 67 Apollo Drive, Rosedale, North Shore 0632, New Zealand
(a division of Pearson New Zealand Ltd.)
Penguin Books (South Africa) (Pty.) Ltd., 24 Sturdee Avenue,
Rosebank, Johannesburg 2196, South Africa

Penguin Books Ltd., Registered Offices:
80 Strand, London WC2R 0RL, England

The scanning, uploading, and distribution of this book via the Internet or via any other
means without the permission of the publisher is illegal and punishable by law. Please
purchase only authorized electronic editions and do not participate in or encourage
electronic piracy of copyrighted materials. Your support of the author's rights is appreciated.

SPEED RACER MOVIE: © Warner Bros. Entertainment Inc.
SPEED RACER: ™ Speed Racer Enterprises, Inc.
WB SHIELD: ™ & © Warner Bros. Entertainment Inc.
(s08)

www.speedracerthemovie.com

The publisher does not have any control over and does not assume
any responsibility for author or third-party websites or their content.

Used under license by Penguin Young Readers Group.
All rights reserved. Published by Price Stern Sloan, a division of Penguin Young
Readers Group, 345 Hudson Street, New York, New York 10014. *PSS!* is a registered
trademark of Penguin Group (USA) Inc. Printed in the U.S.A.

ISBN 978-0-8431-3210-6   10 9 8 7 6 5 4 3 2 1

Speed's hands tightened around the steering wheel as he plowed into the next turn on the racetrack. He passed a car on his left and two more on his right. He slammed the gearshift into fourth, zipping by yet another car. Then he floored the accelerator as he neared the jump ramp. As the Mach 6 launched into the air and soared high above the track, the force shoved Speed back against his seat. Speed's chest pulled against his safety belt as he slammed back to the ground. His tires found traction against the racetrack just in time to make the next turn. Once through the hairpin curve, he roared past two more cars as if they were parked.

Speed Racer was at one with the Mach 6. The T-180-class race car was a model of precision craftsmanship and modern technology. Through his helmet he could hear the churning pistons and the ratcheting gears. With his entire body, from his hands on the wheel to his back on the seat, he sensed everything else. Speed felt the vibration of the motor, the spinning tires against the track, and the air blowing against the car's aerodynamic body. And if all that wasn't enough, he was even wearing his lucky red socks. If he had to, Speed could drive this race with his eyes closed.

Although Speed was an advanced driver for a young adult, he wasn't always this good. Luckily, he had a great teacher. As he took another turn, Speed thought back to several years ago, when racing was in his blood . . . but not yet in his heart.

A much younger Speed Racer sat in a filled classroom taking an exam. Only the sounds of quiet scribbling and the occasional sigh could be heard. His teacher, Ms. Waterstraat, scanned the class over the rims of her glasses.

Barely half the ovals on his answer sheet were filled in. And even those were scarred with eraser marks from where he had changed his answer several times. Speed's pencil was busy scribbling, but not on the test form. He drew a small doodle of a race car on a scratch sheet of paper. Once he added the finishing touches to its thick tires, he rubbed his eyes. He returned his attention to the next test question.

Grace buys a bag of 240 jelly beans. There are 35 yellow ones, 52 red ones, 63 green ones, 26 white ones, 41 blue ones, and 40 black ones. If Grace wants to eat one of each while keeping her eyes closed, what is the minimum number she will have to eat?

Speed sighed. Why would anyone want to eat jelly beans with their eyes closed? *He glanced up at the clock. There was only a minute left before the bell rang, and Speed still had half of his test to complete.*

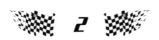

2

That wasn't even enough time for Speed to figure out the answer to the jelly bean question. Speed glanced at the doodle of the race car and smiled. He quickly filled in the remaining dots on his test. He finished just as the bell rang.

"All right, pencils down," said Ms. Waterstraat. "Bring your tests to my desk."

The room was alive with activity as everyone prepared to leave. Speed snatched up his backpack and was the first to reach the teacher's desk. He didn't stop as he tossed the sheet on her desk and headed for the door.

"Speed Racer, slow down!" ordered the teacher.

Speed didn't listen. He hit the door and ran down the hallway. He wanted to get out of the school before his teacher noticed that he used the rest of the answer bubbles to spell out "Go, Rex, Go!"

As Speed ran outside, he saw his brother Rex standing in front of the Mach 5, the very same car that Speed had been doodling. Rex looked like a taller, older version of Speed with the same short brown hair and green eyes. Speed opened the door and climbed into the passenger seat. He had his safety belt buckled before Rex even made it back to the driver's side.

Rex chuckled. "I take it you're ready to go?"

Speed nodded as his older brother got behind the wheel and drove away from the school.

Speed gazed out at the surrounding traffic. All

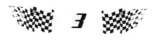

5

of the sleek cars interested young Speed—but none as much as the one he was riding inside.

Their father, Pops Racer, had designed the Mach 5. It was one of a kind, inside and out. Its glossy white body flowed gracefully like ocean waves. The hood and front fenders jutted ahead of the car to form three elegant points. Its two seats were covered in red leather. Painted across the hood was a matching red M, and the number 5 adorned both doors. There was no other car quite like it.

Rex shifted into third gear as they pulled onto the busy street. He turned to Speed and smiled. "So, how was school?"

"Fine," replied Speed. "Are you going to the track?"

Rex tightened his lips, not answering.

"Mom said you were," Speed said. "You don't have to drop me off. I could just go with you."

Rex shook his head. "No way. Pops would kill me."

"He doesn't have to know," said Speed. "I wouldn't say anything. Nobody will know. Come on, please, Rex, please!"

Rex stared at the road ahead and didn't reply. For a minute, Speed wondered if he pushed his brother too far. Finally, Rex turned to Speed. "Are you wearing the socks?"

A grin spread across Speed's face as he put his feet on the dashboard. He pulled back both his pant legs to reveal his lucky red socks.

"You roll us again and this will be the last time," said Rex. "Deal?"

"Deal," Speed agreed.

A few minutes later, Rex and Speed arrived at the Thunderhead Raceway. Speed sat in the stands while his brother took several laps around the twisting, looping track. Speed loved watching his brother drive. But there was one thing he loved more—driving himself. Luckily, as the sun began to set, Speed got his chance.

Speed sat in his brother's lap and steered the car around the track. The wheel vibrated in Speed's hands as they sped into a turn that took them up a vertical wall.

"Feel that shimmy?" asked Rex. "That's your hind legs trying to outrun your front."

Speed tightened his grip. "What do I do?"

"Stop steering and start driving," Rex replied. "This isn't a dead piece of metal. A car's a living, breathing thing. She's alive. You can feel her talking to you, telling you what she wants, what she needs. You just have to listen."

Speed brought the car out of the turn and into the straightaway. They barreled toward the biggest jump in the track.

"Close your eyes and listen," Rex instructed. Speed glanced at his brother in disbelief. Rex smiled. "They say that Ben Burns drove the last lap of the '68 Vanderbilt Cup with his eyes closed."

"No way!" said Speed.

"No? Well maybe you can't hear it then," Rex reached up and took the wheel. "Maybe you ought to start hitting those textbooks."

Speed pushed Rex's hands out of the way and closed his eyes. "No! I hear it! I hear it!"

Rex chuckled. "That so? Okay, Mr. Burns, you tell me when to punch it for the jump."

Speed knew they were speeding toward a huge jump. To make it over, a driver would have to hit the gas pedal at just the right moment. Speed could picture the ramp getting closer and closer.

"Now?" asked Rex.

His eyes still shut, Speed shook his head no.

Speed concentrated on the engine pulsing, the wind whistling around the body of the car, and buzz of the tires on the track. The sounds blended perfectly as if they were instruments in a symphony. They seemed to whisper to Speed, telling him everything he needed to know.

"Now!" yelled Speed. He opened his eyes.

Rex floored the gas as they hit the bottom of the ramp. The car picked up speed as the two drivers were shoved backward. A second later, the race car flew off the ramp and into the air. A perfect jump!

Speed glanced up at the empty stands flying by. He knew that one day they would be filled with excited fans . . . fans cheering just for him.

Chapter 2

Trixie cheered along with the rest of the fans at the Thunderhead Raceway. The crowd's roar grew as Speed and the other racers zipped by. The cars moved so fast, a gust of wind blew across the spectators. Trixie wiped a strand of her short black hair from her eyes and cheered louder. She was just as excited as everyone else, if not more. And the only thing louder than the crowd's cheers were the announcers' voices blaring from the loudspeakers.

"Local fan favorite, Speed Racer, is gobbling up the track," said an announcer. "He's slipping by car after car."

"No one's able to lay a glove on this kid," added a second commentator. "Clearly a rising star with several big wins since turning pro."

"He still remains without a major sponsor," said the first man. "But a win tonight could put him within range of qualifying for the Grand Prix."

"Let's hope he doesn't make the same mistakes as his brother Rex," said the second.

Trixie tried to tune out the announcers' voices. She was there to watch a race, not listen to two guys tell her how great her boyfriend was. She already knew that.

Her heart beat quickly as she watched Speed

maneuver the Mach 6 through the pack of cars. Full of twists, turns, and jumps, the Thunderhead Raceway was a dangerous track. But Speed had the skills to be a top driver in the league, and he had driven this course many times before.

"Jeepers! Look at him go!" yelled Spritle, Speed's little brother. He turned to his pet chimpanzee, Chim-Chim. "He's going to win, I just know it!" The little boy and the chimp exchanged a high five.

Standing beside them were Mom and Pops Racer. They were just as excited to be watching this race as their youngest son. Pops had designed and built the Mach 6. Even though he wasn't wearing a headset and had no direct communication to his son, Pops yelled advice, anyway.

"Watch this next turn," he shouted. "You have to come at it from the outside!"

Trixie smiled as she turned her attention back to the blur of red and white that was the Mach 6. She thought back to when she had first met the entire Racer family. It was quite an exciting introduction to the world of racing.

A much younger Trixie walked down the sidewalk with a few girls from her class. She didn't know why she hung around them. They usually didn't have anything nice to say about anyone.

"My daddy told me he used to work for the Mishida Motorworks, but he quit," said the blond pack leader. She was talking about Pops Racer. His

tinkering in the garage made him famous around the entire neighborhood. "My daddy said that was a completely crazy thing to do," she continued. "He says the whole family is crazy."

"Speed's not crazy," said Trixie. The words were out of her mouth before she had time to think about it. Speed and Trixie were in the same class, but barely knew each other. However, Trixie was certain there was something very special about Speed.

The girls burst into laughter. "No, he's just dumb," said the blond girl. "Probably the dumbest kid in school." She turned to one of the other girls and said, "Ms. Waterstraat had me alphabetize our tests and you wouldn't believe what that moron did."

Trixie couldn't stand it any longer. She balled up a fist and planted it square in the girl's face, sending her falling to the sidewalk.

As the other girls knelt to help her, a shrill whine filled the air. Just then Speed Racer barreled around the corner driving a red and white go-cart. He wore an oversized white helmet, and there was a small brown box in the passenger seat.

As he drove by, his head turned and his eyes met Trixie's. Her breath caught in her chest and she gave Speed a small smile. Speed started to smile back, but he kept his eyes on her a bit too long. His go-cart jumped the curb and tore through a row of bushes.

"Speed!" yelled Trixie as she ran after him.

She dashed through the bushes and saw Speed

sprawled out on the ground. His go-cart lay on its side, wheels still spinning.

Trixie scrambled down the hill. "Are you all right?" she asked when she got to his side.

"Who are you?" asked Speed. His head swayed a bit. Trixie actually caught herself hoping he had bumped his head. She hoped that's why he didn't know who she was.

"I'm Trixie," she replied. "I'm in your class."

"Oh, yeah," said Speed as he slowly got to his feet. He looked at her, smiled, and quickly looked away. He bent and righted his go-cart. "Hey, would you like to see my car collection?" He picked up the small brown box off the ground.

Trixie bit her lower lip and grinned. "I'd love to."

Trixie rode in the seat behind Speed as they tore through the neighborhood. Speed drove as if he were in a major race. Trixie held on tightly as he took the corners. It felt as if they turned on only two wheels.

When they reached the Racer house, Speed pulled into the driveway. He skidded to a stop in front of the open garage door. Inside, two men worked on a beautiful white race car. The older of the men lifted his head from under the car's hood as they arrived. He was heavyset and had a bushy mustache. Everyone in the neighborhood knew who he was— Pops Racer, Speed's dad.

The younger man slid out from under the car and got to his feet. He looked a lot like Speed, but

older. Trixie, and anyone who watched racing, knew exactly who he was. He was the famous young race car driver, Rex Racer.

Speed cut the engine and climbed out of the go-cart. "Hey, Rex. Hey, Pops."

"Hey, Speedy," said Rex.

"Who's your friend?" asked Pops.

"Trixie," replied Speed. "She's in my class."

Trixie stepped out of the cart and waved. "Hi."

Pops smiled and nodded. "Pleasure to meet you."

Speed took the box from Trixie. "Hey, Pops, a guy wanted me to give this to you." He handed him the package. "He said he was a big fan."

"A fan, is it?" He turned the parcel over in his hands. "Not often we get such devoted fans around here." He winked at Trixie before turning back to Speed. "So where is this guy?"

"He was in a hurry," replied Speed. "And he drove a '68 Fendersin. Sweet set of wheels."

"A '68 Fendersin?" asked Rex frantically. He took the box and held it to his ear. "It's ticking!"

Rex shoved the box into the go-cart and jammed it against the accelerator. With a loud whine, the go-cart shot down the driveway. No sooner had it hit the street when . . . KABOOM! The cart exploded and a huge fireball filled the street. A blast of heat washed over Trixie's face. The racing world was more exciting than she'd ever imagined.

"Cool beans!" she said.

Chapter 3

Back on the Thunderhead Raceway, the Mach 6 shuttered as another car bumped it. Speed was careful not to jerk the wheel in response. He knew that even the slightest turn at such a high speed could mean disaster. Instead, Speed carefully adjusted the wheel as he pressed the accelerator. Speed didn't take the other driver's aggressive racing personally. Cars slamming into one another was common during a race. And as a result a good driver not only had to keep track of his own car, but also the others around him. Luckily, Speed had help in that department.

"Heads-up, Speed," came Sparky's voice in his headset. "Seven o'clock. I got Snake drafting Pitter-pat."

Speed glanced at his rearview mirror. He saw an orange-and-black car drafting a ways behind him. Drafting was a common practice in racing. It meant that one car followed very closely behind as a way to reduce wind resistance. Speed recognized the orange-and-black car immediately. It belonged to one of his longtime rivals, Snake Oiler.

"I got him," Speed replied.

"I figure he'll slingshot after you in the next turn," predicted Sparky.

"I'm ready," said Speed.

Speed learned a long time ago that a good racer not only needed a good car, but also a first-rate support crew. Luckily, he had the best. His dad designed and built the Mach 6, while his mechanic, Sparky, helped him maintain it. During the race, Sparky stayed in the pit area and watched the race through a pair of binoculars. For Speed, it was like having eyes in the back of his head.

Speed led the pack as he rocketed into the next turn. He chanced a glance at his rearview mirror. Just as Sparky predicted, Snake made his move. Using the draft from the car ahead of him, Snake performed a slingshot maneuver. While the car ahead blocked some of the wind resistance, Snake was able to pour on the speed. However, as the rest of the cars kept low in the turn, Snake's car went high. He ricocheted off the top guardrail and careened toward the Mach 6. If Speed jerked the wheel to get out of Snake's way, he would surely lose control and crash.

Luckily, he had another option. He pressed a button on his steering wheel. With a loud ratcheting sound, the Mach 6's jacks extended and lifted it off the ground and into the air. While Speed was airborne, Snake's car zoomed underneath the Mach 6, but Snake was going too fast. Just as Speed lowered the jacks, Snake spun out of control and smashed into the lower guardrail. He bounced off and hurled back toward the Mach 6. But Speed knew just how to deal

with Snake. Speed maneuvered his car so he could bump Snake away from him. With the grace of a bullfighter, Speed sent Snake's car spinning back into the pack of cars. A fiery explosion filled Speed's rearview mirrors. Lucky for Snake, all race cars are equipped with kwik-save, expanding foam that protects drivers during a crash. The driver then bounces to safety inside a rubber cocoon.

"Great move," said Sparky. "But you may want to back off on this next—"

Speed cut him off. "Not this time." He shoved the accelerator pedal to the floorboard. He was in the lead and was going to stay that way.

Speed grit his teeth as the track shot straight up into a twisted loop. The g-force he felt as he accelerated was tremendous. It shoved his body firmly to the seat and pressed against his chest. Speed felt as if all the air was being forced from his lungs. As the track finally leveled out, the pressure eased. Speed took a breath. If he kept the lead and this speed, he would break the record his brother had set on this very track several years before.

"Holy, cannoli, Speed," came Sparky's voice through the headset. "Do you know how close you are to breaking Rex's record?"

"Yeah, Sparky," Speed replied. "Yeah, I do."

As Speed held his lead, he thought back to the last time he had seen his big brother. Unfortunately, it wasn't the fondest of memories.

Chapter 4

A much younger Speed Racer sat on his brother's bed. He watched in disbelief as Rex packed clothes into a large black bag.

"Can I go with you?" asked Speed.

Rex zipped the bag shut. "Not this time, Speedy."

"When are you coming back?" asked Speed.

"I don't know," said Rex as he threw the bag's strap over one shoulder. He turned toward the door, and then stopped. "Hey, there's something I want you to have," said Rex. He dug into his jeans pocket, pulled out a small key ring, and held it out.

Speed's chest tightened. "But the Mach 5's your car!"

Rex placed the keys in Speed's hand. "Not anymore." He put down the bag and sat on the bed. "Look, Speed. One day people might say things about me. No matter what they say, I hope you never believe them."

"I won't," said Speed. He wasn't sure what Rex was talking about. And he didn't really care. All that mattered now was that his big brother was leaving.

Rex tousled Speed's hair, got up, and grabbed his bag. Speed followed his brother out into the living room.

Pops stood there with his arms crossed over his chest. "So, you're quitting?"

"I have to," said Rex.

"No you don't," growled Pops. "This is a choice. You're selling out, walking away from everything we've built here."

Rex pushed past Pops. "I'm done arguing with you, Pops." He strode toward the front door.

"Don't you walk away from me!" yelled Pops.

Rex put a hand on the doorknob. "You can't tell me what to do. It's my life to live."

"If you walk out that door," warned Pops. He pointed a threatening finger at Rex. "You better never come back!"

Tears streamed down Speed's cheeks as he waited for Rex's reply. In that moment it was as if time had frozen. Maybe Rex would stay. Maybe he and Pops would make up and everything would be fine.

Speed was crushed when Rex opened the door and walked away forever.

Not long after Rex left, Rex's warning to Speed came true. Racing commentators called for Rex to be suspended or thrown out of racing altogether. They said he intentionally wrecked drivers who were favored to win. Some said he was one of the dirtiest drivers in racing. Others tied him to organized crime. However, Speed kept his promise. He refused to believe any of those things. As Speed watched Rex race on TV, he knew that Rex must have had a good *reason for driving the way he did.*

Then one night the unthinkable happened. Speed and his family were gathered around the television watching Rex drive in the Casa Cristo 5000, one of the most winding and treacherous roads ever raced. The course took drivers through extreme terrains like desert wastelands, jagged mountain ranges, and frozen ice caves. Speed and his family watched in horror as a ball of fire erupted on the screen. Rex had been involved in a fiery crash in the ice caves.

The commentators called it the worst crash in racing history. They said Rex didn't escape the wreck. Speed felt numb as he watched the flames dance across the screen.

Back in the race at the Thunderhead Raceway, Speed shook his head as if to clear away the rotten memories. Speed didn't have time for those. He was about to win the race and beat his brother's record.

After the final turn, the finish line came into view. A man holding the checkered flag was perched above the track. Soon, the Mach 6 would pass beneath him and Speed Racer would win the race. He would pull into the victory lane and drink from the traditional ice-cold bottle of milk, like all winners before him.

But as Speed neared the finish line, he let off the accelerator just a tiny bit. It was so subtle that no one would have ever known. But Speed had slowed down just enough to make sure that he didn't break his brother's record.

Chapter 5

"Come on, Champ," said Speed's mom the next morning. "Rise and shine."

Speed opened his eyes and saw his mother leaning through his bedroom doorway. He blinked and slowly sat up. "I'm up, I'm up," he muttered.

She smiled and disappeared back into the hallway.

Speed moved considerably slower than the day before. He shuffled out of his bedroom and down the hallway. He yawned as he tried to shake the sleep from his head. Other race winners, driving for bigger sponsors, might have been groggy from being up all night at a victory party. Not Speed. He, Pops, and Sparky had been up late going over the Mach 6. They ran tests and examined the engine. They broke down the effects that the race had had on the car and talked about ways that Speed could race even better next time. That's how things worked at Racer Motors. And Speed wouldn't have it any other way.

In the living room, Spritle and Chim-Chim watched Saturday morning cartoons. An animated hero filled the screen as he defeated the villain. Wearing matching pajamas, Spritle and Chim-Chim acted out what was happening on-screen as they

jumped up and down on the couch.

Just then Mom Racer marched into the living room. She zeroed in on Spritle and Chim-Chim. "What are you two doing?"

Spritle froze. "Nothing."

"Is this the same *nothing* that broke my last couch?" she asked.

Simultaneously Spritle and Chim-Chim hopped down. "No, that was a *totally* different nothing," said Spritle. Chim-Chim nodded his head in agreement.

Mom Racer shook her head. "Wash up, and tell your father breakfast is ready."

Spritle and Chim-Chim ran down the hall. "Breakfast is ready!" Spritle yelled.

They burst into the kitchen, followed by Pops and Sparky. As usual, Sparky's orange cap was a bit askew and stained with grease.

The kitchen became quiet as everyone dug into their pancakes. After a few bites, Sparky picked up the morning paper. He began reading aloud. "'It was a virtuoso display of talent, the likes of which has not been seen at Thunderhead since Rex Racer dropped jaws eight years ago. Now, as we once again pull our collective jaw up from the floor, we have to ask, will it be different this time, or will tragedy—'"

"That's enough of that," Mom Racer said with a frown.

Sparky examined the article again. "I just can't believe there wasn't one mention of Racer Motors in there."

Pops took another bite of his pancakes and said, "That's because the sponsors run the media, Sparky." Unlike most of the other drivers, Speed drove as an independent. He didn't have a huge corporation backing him.

There was a brief knock at the back door as Trixie entered. "Morning, everyone," she said. "Is Speed up yet?"

Speed entered the kitchen and was greeted with the smell of his mother's delicious pancakes. The sweet smell made his eyes open a little wider. He poured himself a glass of juice and sat at the table.

Trixie ruffled Speed's hair as she sat beside him. "Hey, superstar, did you see the papers? They're all in love with you."

"Really?" Speed snatched the paper from Sparky.

"Yeah, but there sure is a lot of speculation about which sponsor's going to pick you up," said Sparky.

"That's silly," Spritle said between chews. "Speed's going to keep driving for Pops."

"Well, that's ultimately for Speed to decide," said Pops.

Before Speed could reply, he noticed something very odd. His glass of juice began to tremble. He leaned forward for a closer look then realized the

entire kitchen table was shaking. Everyone looked around as a low rumble filled the air. As the noise grew louder, the floor beneath them shook. Soon, the entire house was vibrating and the rumble grew to a roar.

"Earthquake!" yelled Spritle. He sprang to his feet. "Quick, under the table!"

"Spritle, calm down!" barked Pops.

"But the kitchen is the most dangerous room during an earthquake!" Spritle dove under the table. Meanwhile, Chim-Chim covered his head with a metal pot for protection.

Just as Speed was about to go and investigate, the rumbling suddenly stopped. Everyone glanced around with confused expressions. Then the silence was broken by the ringing of the doorbell.

Everyone followed Pops as he went to the living room and opened the front door. A well-dressed man stood on the stoop. Behind him, parked on the front lawn, was a huge K-Harrier jet.

"Mr. Racer, I hope you will forgive this imposition." The man spoke with a British accent. He extended a hand to Pops. "I am E.P. Arnold Royalton, Esquire, President and Chairman of Royalton Industries, and it is my honor to meet you." Pops tentatively shook his hand. "Mr. Racer, I have been an ardent admirer of your work for years. I remember the first time I saw the prototype for the Mach 1. I told everyone that it didn't belong on a

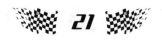

racetrack, it belonged in an art museum."

Pops's uneasiness washed away as a smile stretched across his face. "Yeah, she was a beauty."

Royalton held up a finger. "No, sir. She was a revelation!" He tilted his head and sniffed the air. "Oh, dear. I interrupted your breakfast. Are those pancakes I smell?"

"Why don't you join us, Mr. Royalton?" asked Mom Racer.

Royalton joined the Racer family at the breakfast table. After taking a few bites, he set his fork down and dabbed at his mouth with a napkin. "Now, then," he said, turning to Speed. "We all know the reason I'm here is because of you, Speed. I was watching last night and I have to tell you, young man, you gave me goose bumps. I knew at once, this was no mere driver I was watching. This was an artist!"

Speed glanced at Pops. "A driver is only as good as the car."

Royalton pat him on the shoulder. "I appreciate modesty, Speed. But I don't exaggerate when I say that you are a genius."

"Uh, thanks," said Speed.

The man glanced at Mr. and Mrs. Racer. "I imagine the phone has been ringing off the hook."

Sprite crossed his arms and said, "Speed's not interested in driving for you or any other sponsor." Chim-Chim crossed his arms, too.

Royalton glanced at Speed and then pointed at Spritle. "Is this your manager then?"

"That's Spritle. He's our youngest," said Speed's mother.

Royalton nodded at Spritle. "Nice to meet you, youngster."

Spritle and Chim-Chim glanced at each other, and then back at the man. "We got our eye on you, Mr.," said Spritle.

Royalton chuckled. "Excellent. The first thing I want to make perfectly clear is that I have no intention whatsoever of trying to get Speed away from Racer Motors." He stood and walked around the table. "What you have here is what teams spend years and millions of dollars trying to achieve: chemistry." He gestured to Pops and Sparky. "Car designer, mechanic, and driver all coming together in perfect harmony. I wouldn't dare touch a thing."

"Well, excuse me for asking, but then what do you want?" asked Speed.

"To help," he replied. "I want to make sure you have access to whatever resources you need to continue doing exactly what you are doing."

Pops rubbed the back of his neck. "I assume, Mr. Royalton, that you are not talking about charity."

Royalton chuckled. "I like when my *partners* have a sense of humor. And that's just what I'm talking about." He splayed his hands out before him. "A partnership. An alliance between your

23

amazing family and mine. That's exactly what Royalton Industries is to me, a family. Like yours. Just a little bigger."

"No offense, Royalton, but Racer Motors runs as an independent," said Pops.

Royalton shook his head. "None taken. I completely understand." He paced toward Pops. "You may think of R.I. as a huge corporate conglomerate but I built it from the ground up. So while Royalton Industries may look like a major sponsor to you, it remains, in my heart, as independent as the first day I quit my job at GloBocom to work for myself."

Royalton moved toward the kitchen door and spun around. "Now . . ." He clapped his hands together. "I've had this wonderful opportunity to meet your family. All I'm asking for is the chance to introduce you to mine."

Speed looked around at his family. His eyes met Trixie's. She shrugged her shoulders as if to say, "It couldn't hurt." Speed wondered if that really was true.

Chapter 6

Cruncher Block leaned back and looked at Taejo Togokahn. Taejo's face was bruised and swollen. Two of Cruncher's thugs were holding Taejo down.

"I thought we had a deal," said Cruncher. He stood and walked toward Taejo. "I thought we were friends." Cruncher reached down and lifted Taejo's head. Taejo jerked his head from Cruncher's grasp.

Cruncher crouched before him. "Maybe where you come from, this is how you treat your friends," he said. "But around here we don't take kindly to this kind of thing." Cruncher stood up and walked back to his seat. "Problem is, I like you, Taejo," said Cruncher as he pulled out a switchblade knife. With a push of a button, the blade extended. However, instead of using the knife on Taejo, he cut the string that was wrapped around a package on his desk.

"And I got a real soft spot in my heart for that sister of yours," Cruncher said as he unwrapped the package. Inside was a large T-bone steak—raw. "Normally in a situation such as this we would be pouring you a pair of cement shoes, but I think I have another solution."

Cruncher took the steak over to the large fish tank behind his desk. Swimming inside were his pride and joy—a school of piranhas. The large fish

darted back and forth as he drew closer. Their mouths were filled with razor-sharp teeth.

"How are my babies doing?" asked Cruncher. He dangled the steak over the water. "Hungry?"

Cruncher dipped the steak into the tank. The water began to churn and foam as the fish devoured the raw meat. After a few seconds, all that was left was the bone. The fish had stripped it clean.

Cruncher glanced at Taejo, then back to the fish. "I wonder if they're ready for seconds?"

Cruncher's henchmen grabbed Taejo and dragged him toward the tank.

"No!" yelled Taejo.

"Don't worry, it only hurts for a few seconds," said one of the thugs. "Then you'll probably black out."

"No, please!" shouted Taejo.

"It's going to be hard to drive without a hand," said the other thug.

Cruncher grabbed Taejo's wrist. He forced his hand toward the top of the tank. He leaned close to Taejo's ear. "And if you even think about telling anyone about our deal, your sister will go in here."

Suddenly, the room was bathed in crimson as a red light flashed from the ceiling. Cruncher growled as he released Taejo and moved to his desk. He picked up the phone. "What?!"

"Someone's tailing us," said one of Cruncher's guards.

"Is it him?" asked Cruncher.

"It could be," the guard replied.

Cruncher motioned for the boys to check out the back. The two thugs threw Taejo into the chair and moved toward the end of the office. One of the thugs slid open a small hatch and peered outside to the highway.

This was no ordinary office. Cruncher and his men had set up shop in the trailer of a semitruck. But what was the use in having a mobile office if it didn't keep you from being interrupted during important business meetings?

"Can you see him yet?" asked Cruncher.

"Not yet," the thug replied.

Cruncher pushed a button on his desk and a video monitor rose into view. Now he could see what his henchman was looking at.

Cruncher saw the familiar yellow car appear on the screen with a number 9 painted on the hood. Everyone in racing knew who drove the Shooting Star. He pressed a button and the camera zoomed in on the driver. The man wore a black helmet with a large *X* across the front. As usual, he also wore a visor, hiding his identity.

"It's him!" said Cruncher. "It's Racer X!"

Racer X pressed the accelerator. He hoped he wasn't too late to save Taejo. If Cruncher had the young driver in his mobile office, then there was no telling what shape he'd be in.

As Racer X closed the gap between himself and Cruncher, several small slots opened on the trailer. Racer X swerved as he saw gun barrels poke out. He pressed a button and a clear canopy appeared over his open cockpit. Bullets ricocheted off the hard surface.

As Racer X pulled alongside the truck, it swerved toward him. Racer X hit the brakes and his car slowed. The truck pulled away, missing him entirely.

Suddenly, a large gun dropped from the bottom of the truck. Its barrel turned toward his car and erupted. A stream of bullets flew toward him as the machine gun opened fire. Racer X jerked the wheel to get clear of the attack. The hail of bullets sparked across the pavement after him. But as Racer X dodged the attack, the gunman misfired and hit one of his own tires.

The wheel exploded as black tread flopped away and tumbled down the highway. The gun ceased firing before hitting any other wheels.

This was Racer X's chance. He hit the gas. This time he was able to zoom by. Unfortunately, as he pulled out front, the grill of the truck retracted, revealing three rows of rockets. One of them fired, zooming right at him. Racer X jerked the wheel and the missile flew past him. It blew up a tree farther up the road. He swerved again as another rocket zoomed by. It hit the road ahead. Racer X barely

missed the huge crater and fireball.

Now Racer X had to do more than just dodge Cruncher's attacks. It was time to go on the offensive. Racer X hit the brakes, letting the big rig pull up alongside him. As he did, machine guns of his own erupted from the Shooting Star. They riddled the top of the truck with holes. He purposely aimed high so no one would get hurt. He didn't want to chance hitting Taejo.

This seemed to take the fight out of them. They slowed and pulled to the side of the highway. To the masked racer's dismay, the truck didn't stop completely. The back doors opened and Taejo was thrown from the trailer. Racer X had to slam on the brakes to keep from running him down.

As Cruncher's semi pulled away, Racer X stepped out of the car. He helped Taejo to his feet and into the passenger seat. It looked as if they worked him over pretty good. Once inside, Racer X pulled back onto the highway.

"Thank you," said Taejo. "You saved my life."

Racer X kept his eyes on the road. "You thought you could take on the cartel? Well, you can't. Not without help."

Taejo looked away. "I don't know what you're talking about."

"You won the Cortex Invitational and you weren't supposed to," said Racer X. "You did it to save Togokahn Motors."

"It has belonged to my family for five generations," said Taejo.

"And now someone else wants it," said Racer X. "The only way you can stop it from happening is to talk to the authorities."

Taejo lowered his head. "There is nothing to say."

Racer X sighed. "You've been on Cruncher Block's leash for so long maybe you forgot how it feels to stand up and be a man. The only way you'll ever stop these people is to bring them to justice."

"Justice?" Taejo laughed. "That's a commodity I don't waste my money on."

Racer X slammed on the brakes. The car skidded to a stop. He turned and glared at Taejo. "Get out."

Taejo opened the door and climbed out of the car. He slammed the door behind him. "I'll see you at Fuji," Taejo smirked.

"You won't finish," replied Racer X. He opened a console and retrieved one of Inspector Detector's business cards. He held it out to Taejo. "When you lose, if you can still dial a phone, call this number."

When Taejo took the card, Racer X hit the gas. He peeled out, leaving Taejo on the side of the road.

Racer X couldn't believe how stupid the young driver was. He knew from personal experience that you couldn't take on the cartels alone. Racing was a dangerous sport, but some of its seedier elements made it even more hazardous. He only hoped Taejo realized this before it was too late.

Chapter 7

Speed gazed through the glass floor of Royalton's K-Harrier as they flew over Cosmopolis. Even though he'd flown over it several times in Trixie's helicopter, the grand city always amazed him. Glittering towers jutted from the earth in every shape, color, and size. Sparkling logos and icons in dozens of different languages adorned the skyscrapers like name tags. Helicopters buzzed in the sky like bees over a summer field. For someone who did his best work hugging the ground at supersonic speeds, Speed Racer was in awe of the view.

The rest of the group enjoyed the ride as well. They each sat in overstuffed leather seats surrounded by polished wood paneling. The roar of the jet's engines was muffled by the soundproof hull and completely drowned out by the classical music playing through hidden speakers.

Speed's mom gazed at the passing skyscrapers. "I've never flown so low through the city."

Royalton beamed with pride. "Special permit. Only six of them are granted a year."

Meanwhile, Spritle and Chim-Chim stared at a different view. A flight attendant in a crisp uniform opened a panel in front of them. "Take whatever you like," she said, gesturing to a wide selection of candy.

The young boy and chimp glanced at each other with mouths agape. Then they both lunged for the candy. They slapped each other's hands out of the way as they battled for the sweets.

"Spritle!" barked Pops.

With his hands still tangled with Chim-Chim's, Spritle turned to Pops. "But she said we could!"

Pops narrowed his eyes and Spritle sighed. He and Chim-Chim each took only one piece of candy.

"What do you say?" asked Pops.

Spritle smiled at the attendant. "Thank you."

The woman nodded and closed the panel. Spritle and Chim-Chim looked on with wide eyes as their treasure disappeared.

"Hey, there's the Grand Prix Coliseum!" said Sparky. He pointed out the window. The enormous dome nearly filled their entire view. Speed knew a track similar to Thunderhead lay hidden beneath the giant dome, a tangled maze of twists, turns, loops, swirls, and jumps. Only five times bigger.

"My brother's going to win the Grand Prix one day," announced Spritle.

"No doubt in my mind, young man," agreed Royalton. He gave a wide smile. "Given the right circumstances, I have no doubt whatsoever."

Speed glanced at Trixie. She smiled and squeezed his hand.

The jet banked and the coliseum slipped from view. They now stared at a colossal high-rise. A giant R adorned the front and, for a moment, it seemed as if the jet was going to crash right into it. Fortunately, they began to climb vertically. Floors of glass and steel flashed by as they ascended. Once on top of the building, the jet gently touched down on a private landing pad.

After everyone deplaned, they were met by a group of uniformed men and women. Royalton pointed to a beautiful brunette woman in the center. "This is Gennie. She's our Talent Manager. Ask for anything, her job is to make it come true."

Gennie stepped forward and shook Speed's hand. "Hi, Speed. Welcome to Royalton."

She snapped her fingers and a uniformed man rushed up to Speed. He held out a small device that scanned Speed's body. Then the man tapped a few buttons on the device and scurried away.

"What was that all about?" asked Speed.

Royalton put a hand on Speed's shoulder. "To make an informed decision, you'll need to understand how we take care of our drivers."

Gennie waved to someone down a hallway and a long tram emerged. The driver pulled the tram to a stop in front of Speed and the others. Like a small train, there were plenty of seats for everyone.

"All aboard," said Royalton. He took the front seat as everyone piled into the others.

"Cool!" said Spritle as he looked around.

When everyone was seated, the tram pulled into a wide hallway. Uniformed workers riding smaller trams and scooters buzzed about as they drove by. The walls were adorned with signs pointing to various locations within the facility as well as advertisements for Royalton products.

Royalton turned to address the rest of the passengers. "Royalton Tower is the crown jewel among the properties I control. It functions as the corporate headquarters for the top twelve divisions of our parent company. One big industrious family."

They turned a corner and zipped toward two huge double doors. Two large *R*s adorned them.

"Of all the 143 companies that I control, none of them is as dear to my heart as the T-180 division," said Royalton. The doors opened as they neared. "I've always felt that it is impossible to peer into the window of tomorrow without a clear view of the past."

The tram slowed as they drove through a huge auto museum. Every kind of race car Speed had ever heard of or seen was represented. Some hung from the ceiling, while others sparkled under spotlights. Every car from the golden age of racing sat before them.

Spritle pointed in awe. "That's the Crystal Horse with the Apache Super-Charger!"

"Winner of the Grand Prix in '69, '70, and '73,"

added Royalton with more than a little pride.

Spritle shook his head. "Wrong. '72. '71 was the Vundervopper with the K-9 twin turbine. '73 was the Kenobe Motorstar rebuilt with a VC triple chamber."

Royalton was about to reply when Speed held up a hand. "Don't bother," said Speed. "He's never wrong."

The tram left the museum and turned down another long corridor with windows on both sides. It was an observation deck overlooking a huge factory.

A vertical assembly line stretched several stories below them. Robotic arms passed unfinished T-180 race cars to various platforms. Several more robotic arms added parts to the skeletal chassis before moving to another station.

"Our vertically integrated plant is the fastest in the world," boasted Royalton. "From initial carbon bond to finished car in thirty-six hours." He smiled at Pops. "How long does it take at Racer Motors?"

Sparky leaned out of the tram to get a better look. "Several weeks at least."

"This kind of production facility could be at your disposal, Mr. Racer," said Mr. Royalton.

Speed glanced at his father. He could tell Pops was trying to hide his amazement.

The tram motored out of the production plant and entered another windowed corridor. In contrast to the first factory, this one was completely white

and sterile. Huge engine blocks sat on pedestals while robotic arms worked on them like surgeons in an operating room.

"This is our operating theater where our patented Refusion Distributor is installed in the turbine drive," said Royalton.

Sparky pointed at the high-tech engine. "Is that an Inner-Positive Transponder?"

"It is indeed," replied Royalton. "We control the only transponder foundry in the world besides Musha Motors."

This time, both Pops and Sparky leaned in for a closer look. Suddenly, the clear glass turned into a mirror.

"Oops. Sorry," said Royalton. "Trade secrets, you know."

The tram exited the corridor only to stop at another set of double doors. They swung open to reveal a small chamber with doors on the other side. After they drove inside, the doors closed behind them. The driver pressed a button on his console and they began to rise. They hadn't realized it at first, but they were parked inside a large elevator.

"Now, I'll take you up to the Team Royalton training facility," said Royalton.

Moments later, the elevator stopped and the doors in front of them opened. The tram glided into what looked like a different building entirely. Gone were the sterile and industrial hallways. This

part of the facility seemed more like a country club than a factory. Softer light washed over the warmly painted walls and décor.

They rolled past more windows revealing a large gym. Young men and women worked out on state-of-the-art exercise equipment. Some lifted weights while others ran on treadmills.

"As you know, a T-180 driver's got to be in peak physical condition," said Royalton.

The next window showed a giant centrifuge with a cockpit attached at the end of a robotic arm. The large machine spun in circles inside a round room. A helmeted driver sat inside the cockpit.

Royalton pointed to the spinning man. "The best drivers must be able to withstand over four gs in a typical race."

Trixie tapped Speed on the shoulder. "Look," she said, pointing to the opposite wall.

Speed turned to see another testing chamber with a driver strapped to a chair atop a large vibrating machine. He was shaking so hard that Speed wondered if his eyeballs would pop out.

Through the next window, they saw a driver inside a cockpit pressing pedals and shifting gears. Nothing strange about that—except that she was doing it all underwater! Bubbles rose from her helmet as she received air from a large hose.

"The will to win is nothing without the will to prepare," said Royalton. "And at Team Royalton we

prepare our drivers for any eventuality and every possible condition."

The tram reached the end of the corridor and turned toward another set of doors. Royalton leaned toward Speed. "I hope I didn't scare you with how hard we push our team. I just wanted you to see how seriously we are committed to winning."

Speed chuckled. "I get that."

"Good," said Royalton as they passed through the doorway. "But also understand that R.I. isn't all work and no play."

The tram rolled into a huge lounge area. Drivers sat in overstuffed chairs while being served by waiters and waitresses. There was even a gaming area where drivers played pool and other games.

Spritle leaped to his feet, pointing to the game room. "That's Cannonball Taylor!" Speed turned, and sure enough, there was the captain of the Royalton team.

Royalton leaned toward the driver. "Stop the cart." Once they stopped, Royalton climbed out and waved Taylor over. "Jack! Jack, come here. There's someone I want you to meet."

Cannonball Taylor walked over to the tram. Royalton patted him on the shoulder and pointed to Speed. "Speed Racer, allow me to introduce two-time Grand Prix winner, five-time WRL Champion and future Hall of Famer, Jack 'Cannonball' Taylor."

Speed stood and shook his hand. "Honor to meet you."

Cannonball gave a sparkling smile. "Caught that Thunderhead replay. Nice piece of work."

"Wow, thanks," said Speed. He couldn't believe that a Grand Prix winner would have even noticed his driving.

"There was a rumor you might be visiting," said Cannonball.

Speed glanced around. "It's all pretty impressive."

"Only thing I cared about was that wall over there." Taylor pointed to a wall in the lounge. It was covered in medals, plaques, and trophies. "That's what sold me. You want to win in this league, you're talking to the right guy."

Royalton beamed. "Thanks, Jack."

After the tram took them out of the lounge, they were taken to the very top floor of the building—the penthouse. Crisp, modern furniture decorated the luxury suite, and huge windows gave a panoramic view of the city.

Royalton spread his arms wide. "We treat our thoroughbreds the way they deserve to be treated. There's full maid service, of course, with a personal chef and masseuse available 24/7."

Gennie entered, holding a luxurious black suit. She held it out to Speed. "It should be perfect. Try it on."

Speed went to a nearby changing room and put on the suit. It fit his body perfectly. He had never worn a piece of clothing that fit so well. This must have been why he had been scanned when he first got to the building.

When he stepped out in his new clothes, Trixie was the first to react. "Hubba hubba," she said.

"Oh, honey, you look so handsome," said his mother.

"Yeah?" asked Speed.

"Very sharp, Speed," said Royalton. "Suits you perfectly. Regardless of what happens, I want you to keep it as a gift."

"Thanks," said Speed.

The man turned to Speed's parents. "So, Mrs. Racer, what do you think about *my* family? Impressed?"

Mom Racer raised her eyebrows. "You could say that."

"Good. I want you to understand the possibilities that exist for your son right now," said Royalton.

Pops gave a small wince. It didn't go unnoticed by Royalton. "What's wrong, Mr. Racer?"

"To be honest, I'm feeling more intimidated than impressed," Pops replied. He nervously rubbed the back of his neck. "This kind of company scares me. When someone has this kind of money they start thinking that the rules everyone else is playing by don't mean squat to them."

Pops moved over to Speed and put a hand on his shoulder. "However, my sons are the most important thing *I've* ever done in my life. If Speed wants us to figure out some kind of . . . *alliance*, then you can bet we'll be in business."

Royalton smiled and turned to Speed. "So, how are you feeling?"

Speed looked down at his suit then up at the faces of his friends and family. He wasn't sure what to do. "It's all very . . . impressive," he said.

Royalton leaned in. "You think that maybe there's something that could work out here?"

"I guess I'd like to think about it, if I could," said Speed.

Royalton's smile faltered. "This isn't the kind of offer I go around making every day, son."

"I understand that, sir," said Speed. "So if I had to give an answer now, then to be honest—"

"Stop right there," interrupted Royalton. "You're right. You should think about it. I'm sure you're feeling a bit overwhelmed. You should take a little time. Think about what you saw and heard here and we'll get together . . . tomorrow!" He extended a hand. "Deal?"

With a sigh of relief, Speed shook it. "Deal."

Chapter 8

Late that afternoon, Speed and Trixie took the Mach 5 to Inspiration Point to watch the sunset. They often parked up there and talked for hours. However, as red and orange light streaked across the sky, they didn't say much to each other. Speed had a lot on his mind.

Finally, Trixie broke the silence. "You're really considering signing with Royalton?"

"It's tempting," said Speed.

"Why?" she asked.

Speed began to rattle off his *pro* list. "Well, they have a really good team. Cannonball Taylor, Maggie Manifold. They win a lot of majors."

"Since when did winning become so important?" asked Trixie.

"It *is* important," replied Speed. "You have to win if you want to keep driving and that's what I want to do." He sighed. "It's the only thing I really know how to do."

"That's not true," said Trixie.

"But when I'm in the Mach 6, I don't know, everything just makes sense," said Speed.

Trixie took his hand. "Are you saying this doesn't make sense?"

Speed smiled. "Okay, this makes sense, too."

She rested her head on his shoulder. "So you like this?"

"Yeah, this isn't so bad," said Speed.

Trixie playfully slugged his chest. "I was starting to wonder."

"Wonder what?"

"Well, with you so busy becoming Mr. Super Famous Race Car Driver," said Trixie. "I was starting to wonder if you were still interested in this."

"Come on," said Speed. "You know I am."

She rolled her eyes. "Well, sometimes a girl could use a reminder."

"You mean like a new igniter for your helicopter?" asked Speed.

She shook her head. "Nope."

"How about a tire burn that spells out your name?" he asked.

"Warmer."

"Maybe at the end of some big race, when I pull into the victory lane, I should scoop you into my arms," he said dramatically. "And then kiss you with thousands of flashbulbs going off!"

Trixie jolted up. "Would that be so terrible, Mr. Super Famous Race Car Driver?"

"I don't know," Speed shrugged his shoulders. "Maybe we should practice."

Trixie smiled and leaned closer. "Maybe we should."

Just as they were about to kiss, a muffled voice sounded behind them. "Oh man! I'm going to hurl!"

"Spritle?" asked Trixie.

"He did not!" shouted Speed and Trixie as they jumped from the car and headed for the trunk. "Spritle!" they said in unison as they popped the trunk.

Speed's little brother and Chim-Chim were curled inside the trunk. The chimpanzee covered his eyes as if still hiding.

"You sneak!" said Trixie.

"It wasn't my idea!" said the boy.

"Oh no?" asked Speed.

Spritle pointed at Chim-Chim. "It was his!" The chimpanzee shook his head and pointed back at Spritle.

"Wait until we tell Pops," said Trixie.

Spritle stepped out of the trunk. "No! Don't do that! We're sorry. We couldn't sleep. We just wanted to hang out. We didn't know you were going to In-*spew*-ration Point." Spritle pointed a finger at Chim-Chim's shoulder. "By the way, cootie shots!" He pressed his finger against the chimp's arm, pretending to give him a shot. Chim-Chim quickly did the same thing to Spritle.

Speed shook his head. "I'm taking you home."

"Wait, wait, wait," said Spritle. He ducked as Speed closed the trunk. "Can we stop for ice cream first?" he asked with a muffled voice.

44

The next morning, Speed found Pops in the Racer garage. The large bay contained everything a small racing team could need. It was full of parts, equipment, and an extraordinary white race car in the center—the Mach 6. Pops wore a clear face shield as he used an electric sander on the car's front fender. When Speed entered, Pops turned off the power tool.

"Morning, Speed," said Pops.

"Hey, Pops."

"So, today's the big day," his father said as he pulled off the clear mask. He looked his son square in the eyes and sighed. "Look, I know this is a tremendous opportunity for you."

"It could be for you, too," said Speed.

Pops nodded. "Could be, could be. But, regardless, this is really all about you. It's your decision and I want you to know, no matter what you decide, I'm behind you."

Speed smiled. "Thanks, Pops."

Suddenly, the floor began to shake as a few tools rattled off the pegboard. Pops chuckled. "I think your ride is here."

Speed ran to his room, grabbed a closed paper bag, and dashed outside.

Once at Royalton Tower, Speed was escorted directly to Royalton's office. The elevator doors opened, revealing a huge room with a large desk at the other side. Royalton sprang from behind it. "Speed!" he said as he jogged across the room and gave Speed a big hug. "Welcome back!"

Before Speed could respond, the man grabbed him by the arm and pulled him across the room. They stopped at an easel covered with a black silk cloth. "Look at this," said Royalton as he whipped off the silk.

On the easel were prototypes for a new logo featuring two huge *R*s and the words *Royalton's Racer Motors*.

"Uh, wow," said Speed. He hardly knew what to say.

Royalton grinned. "That's what I thought. We're still working on the *R and R* but it's getting there." He ushered him to a cluster of large chairs in the center of the room. "Come. Sit. We can talk logos later."

Speed sat awkwardly in the huge chair. The paper bag rested in his lap. Eyes bright, Royalton could hardly contain his enthusiasm. "Can I get you something to drink?"

"No, I'm okay," said Speed.

Royalton leaned back and looked thoughtful. "So,

I can see you've given some serious thought to this thing."

"Yes, sir," said Speed. "I have."

"Good," said Royalton. "That means that you understand that we are talking about not only your future, but your family's future."

"My family means a lot to me," said Speed.

The man nodded. "I can tell. That's why this is so important. Because *you* can help them. All you have to say is *yes*. That is all I need to hear and I can make so many things happen for you, and your family." He leaned forward. "Are you ready for that? Are you ready to say *yes*, Speed?"

Speed swallowed hard. "This isn't an easy decision for me, Mr. Royalton. For my family, racing is everything." He squirmed in his seat. "I was tooling timing pins with Pops while I was still wearing diapers. For us, there's nothing more perfect than a picnic at Thunderhead. But when my brother died, all that went away. I can't tell you how painful that was. It nearly killed all of us. Especially Pops. He didn't set foot in his shop for over a year."

Speed's mouth went dry. It was difficult talking about his brother. But he had to make Royalton understand where he was coming from. "One night, when I was still pretty young, I couldn't sleep and I went into the living room. There was Pops, in his beat-up robe, watching some old race recordings."

The smile began to fade from Royalton's face. He didn't like where this was going. Still, Speed continued. "So I sat with him watching old Ben Burns coming around the last turn of the '43 Grand Prix. Then Pops started screaming for Burns as he and Stickleton duked it out, heading for the finish. We both cheered our heads off. And when the checkered flag came down, we looked at each other. Right there we realized the naked truth: Racing is in our blood."

Royalton didn't say a word.

"But for Pops, it isn't just a sport," Speed explained. "It's way more important than that. It's like a religion in our house." He held up a hand. "I don't mean to offend you, sir. I do appreciate your offer." He sighed. "It's just . . . after all we've been through, I don't think this kind of deal is right for me."

The smile was now completely gone from Royalton's face. He rolled his eyes. "You poor, naïve, chump."

Chapter 10

Royalton got to his feet and paced around the room. Gone was the kind smile and generous hospitality. The man's brow wrinkled and his eyes shot daggers. Speed got the feeling that this was the true E.P. Arnold Royalton, Esquire.

"I'm going to pretend that I didn't hear that sickeningly sweet story and give you an education," growled Royalton. "At the end of it, if you're smart, you'll thank me, and then you'll *sign* with me."

Royalton marched toward a door and motioned for Speed to join him. They entered a room full of old racing memorabilia. There were several checkered flags, a couple of empty milk bottles, and even a wrecked race car.

Speed followed Royalton past some old photos from the golden age of racing. Classic race cars were on display along with their legendary drivers. Then he led Speed to the mangled mass of metal.

"Interesting that you and your father were so moved by the '43 Prix," said Royalton. "One of the greatest finishes in the history of racing, right? Everyone remembers Burns and Stickleton slugging it out, but who remembers Carl Potts?"

Speed shrugged. He didn't know that name.

"Potts spun out in the second lap," Royalton

explained. "He drove a rebuilt Wittingan for Iodyne Industries." He pointed to the mass of twisted metal. "A forgettable and pathetic finish. So bad that afterward, Iodyne stock dropped six points."

Royalton raised a finger. "But Ben Burns sat guzzling cold, fresh milk in the victory lane. A thousand cameras took his picture and the stock of his sponsor, Sirrus Aeronautics, soared." Royalton beamed. "This put Joel Goldman, the CEO of Iodyne, in the exact position he wanted to be in. Now that his stock was so cheap, he bought controlling interest in his own company at a very low price. Then he made a deal with Sirrus that sent Iodyne into the gains record book—the only record book that matters."

Royalton pointed to a window. "Look out that window. Now there isn't a single plane, helicopter, or K-Harrier that isn't powered by Iodyne fuel cells." He leaned closer to Speed. "That's what racing is about. It has nothing to do with cars or drivers. All that matters is power and money."

Speed didn't understand what one wrecked race car had to do with a major business deal. Sure, the big sponsors bought and sold one another all the time. That's why they invested so much time and money into their racers. When the racers won, they made money.

Royalton laughed. "You still don't get it, do you?" he asked. He shook his head in disbelief. "Burns *knew* he was going to win. It was already decided.

Like it always is." Royalton leaned against the piece of smashed metal. "A week before the Prix, all the major players meet to negotiate the finish order of the Grand Prix. No race is more important and no race is more controlled!"

Speed couldn't believe what he was hearing. Ben Burns, his hero, knew he was going to win? All the racers knew? That was impossible.

Royalton ran a hand over the hunk of wrecked race car. "That's why I paid three million dollars for this burnt and twisted piece of metal. Because it reminds me of what really matters. This is the true heart of racing, boy!"

Speed was speechless as Royalton led him out of the trophy room. "You don't know how many times I have seen that same cow-eyed look of disbelief. Every bumpkin who comes in from the sticks looks exactly like you do now." Royalton crossed to his desk and sat down. "I won't bother proving it to you. If you walk away from me, if you walk out on this deal, you'll know how true it is soon enough."

He picked up a thick bundle of paper and a pen. "So, are you ready to put away your toys and grow up? Are you ready to make more money in one year than your father made in his whole life? Are you ready to become a real race car driver?" He held out the bundle and pen. "Then sign that contract!"

Speed could not, *would not* believe what Royalton told him. All he wanted to do was drive a race car.

He wanted to test his skill against some of the biggest names in racing. But how could he do that if the entire thing was rigged? How could he ever win a major race if the sponsors didn't approve it first? He grabbed the paper bag from his chair and tossed it to Royalton.

"What's this?" asked Royalton. He opened the bag and pulled out Speed's tailor-made suit.

"If that's your idea of racing, you can keep it," said Speed.

Royalton threw the suit across the room. He leaped to his feet. "Listen to me and listen good, kid, because I'm going to give you one more history lesson. You're going to race Fuji, right? You'll race and you'll try to prove that everything I've said is a lie. But no matter how well you drive, you won't win. You won't place." He slammed a fist against his desk. "I guarantee you won't even *finish* the race."

Speed shook his head in disbelief. Royalton couldn't control what he did on the track. Speed turned to leave.

Royalton yelled louder. "After that, there'll be a lawsuit against your father's designs. The legitimacy of the lawsuits won't matter. They'll be enough to discredit his company. Within a year he'll file for bankruptcy. Then you and your pathetic family will be history."

"Pops was right," said Speed. "You are the devil." And with that, Speed walked out the door.

Chapter 11

The next week, Speed found himself behind the wheel on the Fuji Helexicon track, trying desperately to prove Royalton wrong. The track weaved in and out of the lush tropical landscape set against the ocean, with sequins of sunlight coming in and out of view. But Speed didn't have time to look at the scenery. He had a race to win.

Fuji Helexicon was more like a roller coaster than a racetrack. Only extreme speed kept a car glued to the track. Luckily, the Mach 6 had plenty.

Throughout the race, Speed had done remarkably well. He'd avoided several crashes and slowly made his way through the pack of cars. At last, he closed in on the lead car—Gray Ghost.

Suddenly Speed was jolted as a car slammed into him. Speed glanced at the car and saw it edge away from him only to come sliding back for another attack. Speed hit the gas and swerved into the oncoming car. Hitting the other car just right, Speed sent it spiraling back into the pack of cars behind him. The other cars swerved away as the attacking car slid into the rail and exploded. The driver's kwik-save cocoon bounced away as bits of his smashed car rained down on the other racers.

Speed turned his attention back to Gray Ghost.

Speed's body pulled against the seat belt as he accelerated into the next turn. He was about to catch up with the leader when another car hit him.

"What's going on?" Sparky said into Speed's headset. Speed didn't have time to answer.

Another car came out of nowhere. It rammed the attacking car, knocking it away. Speed knew the driver of that car. It was Racer X, the most notorious driver in racing. Speed didn't know why the masked racer would be helping him. Maybe he wanted to save the Mach 6 from the other cars so he could personally take the Mach 6 out of the race. But Speed wasn't going to stick around to find out.

Speed gunned his engine and caught up with Gray Ghost. The two cars danced around each other as if they were sizing each other up. Speed tried to pass when Gray Ghost threw the first punch. He swerved ahead of Speed. He forced Speed to either fall back or get crunched against the guardrail.

Speed pulled the Mach 6 to the right of Gray Ghost. The gray car swerved to block. Speed jerked the wheel, sending him to Gray Ghost's left. He hit the gas and passed him.

Coming into the next turn, Gray Ghost hit back. He slammed into the back of the Mach 6. Both cars went into a synchronized spin. Speed fought to regain control. When he finally had the car facing the right direction, Gray Ghost had taken the lead.

Speed was about to make another move when

yet another car slammed into him. Speed turned, expecting to see Racer X. Instead, he saw the same car that attacked him earlier. The driver grinned as he shoved Speed into the guardrail.

"Get out of there!" yelled Sparky.

Just as Speed hit the accelerator, he felt something slam against the bottom of his car. He tried to pull away but he only kept pace with the car beside him. He tried to turn, but the steering wheel was locked. He even tried the brakes. Nothing.

"I can't move," said Speed into his headset. "I think he speared me."

"A spear hook?" asked Sparky. "That's illegal!"

"Yeah, well," said Speed as he struggled against the locked steering wheel. "If it's under the chassis the judges can't see it, can they?"

Speed remained locked with the other car as they sped up a big ramp and into the air. But their awkward aerodynamics made them tumble. As the Mach 6 spun out of control, Speed felt the hook retract. But Speed didn't have enough time to react. Speed's car smacked against the track. A fraction of a second later, the other car slammed on top of the Mach 6. The Mach 6 would never recover from this.

Instantly, a clear shield covered Speed's face. As the kwik-save foam flooded into the cockpit, Speed remembered what Royalton had said. *No matter how well you drive, you won't win. You won't place. I guarantee you won't even finish the race.*

Chapter 12

It seemed that Royalton was determined to make good on both of his threats. The Racer family hadn't been home from Fuji for long when the doorbell rang. Pops opened the door to find a man in a suit with a grim expression.

"Are you Pops Racer of Racer Motors?" asked the man.

"Yes," Pops replied.

The man reached into his coat and produced a folded bundle of papers. He handed them to Pops. "You are hereby served a summons."

"What?" asked Pops. Speed looked at the papers in Pops's hand.

"You are being served for IP infringement by Janus Automakers," said the man.

"That's ridiculous!" said Speed.

The man smirked. "That's for a jury to decide." He turned and strode down the sidewalk.

Once again, Royalton's words echoed in Speed's head. *The legitimacy of the lawsuits won't matter. They'll be enough to discredit his company. Within a year he'll file for bankruptcy. Then you and your pathetic family will be history.*

Pops collapsed into a chair in the living room. "What's going on around here?"

Sparky entered holding a newspaper. "That's not the half of it." He pointed to the bold headline. It read, ANOTHER DIRTY RACER?

Sparky began reading the article. "'Controversy surrounds Racer Motors, now embroiled in IP litigation. And while evidence remains inconclusive whether or not Speed used an illegal device, the events at Fuji Helexicon seem destined to become another mark of shame added to the notorious Racer family legacy. It's a legacy that has forever tainted the integrity of this beloved sport—'"

"Sparky. That's enough," said Mom Racer.

Sparky lowered the paper. "Sorry, ma'am."

"It's all Royalton's fault," said Spritle. "I'm going to send that guy some Chim-Chim cookies." Chim-Chim nodded in agreement. Everyone knew that he wasn't talking about real cookies.

"You'll do no such thing," barked Pops.

"We've got to do something," said Spritle.

Speed hung his head. "This is exactly what he said would happen if I didn't drive for him."

"He actually said that?" asked Sparky.

Speed nodded. "He said it would get worse and worse and by the end of the year you would be filing for bankruptcy, Pops."

"Okay, he's definitely getting some monkey cookies," said Spritle.

"Spritle!" said Mom Racer.

Pops put an arm around Speed's shoulders. "He

was just trying to scare you, son. They tried the same thing with Rex. If it's a fight they want, then a fight they'll get."

"How?" asked Speed. "What can we do? How can we fight this?"

"The truth will come out," Pops assured him.

"The truth?" asked Speed. He shook off Pops's arm and stormed to his room. "Don't be naïve."

Speed marched straight to the poster of Ben Burns hanging over his bed. It showed a young driver drinking cold milk at the finish line of the '43 Grand Prix. He ripped it from the wall and tore it in half. Then he plopped onto his bed. He felt trapped and helpless.

Moments later there was a tap at the door as his mother poked her head inside. "Speed, are you okay?"

He ran his fingers through his hair. "I don't know."

She sat beside him, pulling his head onto her shoulder. "It'll be okay. We'll get through it."

"I don't know, Mom," said Speed. "I might've really messed things up."

"How?" she asked.

"By not joining Royalton."

"Don't be silly," she said. "You never would've been happy driving for that terrible man."

Speed raised his head. "But maybe racing isn't about being happy. Maybe Royalton's right and it's all about business and anyone who doesn't

understand that is just a chump."

She cupped his chin. "Now you listen to me, young man. What you do behind the wheel of a race car has nothing to do with business. When I watch you do some of the things you do, I feel like I'm watching someone paint or play music. But then there are other times when you just take my breath away. And it's at those moments, when I feel your father's chest swell."

"Really?" he asked.

"Speed, I am so proud to be your mother. And even though your father doesn't say it, he is, too." She got to her feet and headed for the door. "Don't worry. We'll figure this out. We just have to stick together. Something good will happen. You'll see."

Just then, the doorbell rang.

"What now?" asked Speed as he sprang out of bed. He ran past his mother and into the living room just as Spritle opened the front door. On the doorstep stood Inspector Detector. Every racer knew him. He worked for the CIB, the Central Investigation Bureau. The Racer family had gotten to know him all too well during the investigation of Rex's accident. However, it wasn't the sight of the inspector that took Speed's breath away. It was the man standing behind him—Racer X.

"Racer *Hex*!" yelled Spritle. "The Harbinger of Boom! Run for your lives!" He slammed the door in the men's faces.

Chapter 13

"What are you two squawking about?" asked Pops as he stormed into the room.

Spritle and Chim-Chim dove behind the couch. "Whatever you do, don't open that door!"

Pops ignored Spritle's warning. "Inspector Detector?"

"Good morning, Mr. Racer," said the inspector. "I know it's been a long time."

"Ten years," said Pops.

"Yes. I'm sorry for this intrusion, but I was hoping to have a word with you." He glanced at Speed. "And you, too."

Pops seemed reluctant to let them in the house. He shifted his gaze to the man standing behind the inspector. Even away from the racetrack, Racer X still wore his signature black racing suit with the helmet and visor that covered everything on his face but his nose and mouth.

"It's important," the inspector added.

Pops gave in and motioned for the two men to come inside and sit down. As Mom Racer served coffee and cookies, Speed couldn't help but think this was all more than a little surreal.

The inspector politely sipped his drink, then got down to business. "We've been after Royalton for

years for dozens of corporate crimes, including WRL fixing. Unfortunately, we haven't had the evidence we needed to convict him. Until now."

Speed's mother handed Racer X a cup of coffee. "Here you are, Mr. X."

Spritle and Chim-Chim poked their heads out from behind the couch. "What's he doing here?" asked Spritle.

"Racer X works closely with our World Racing League corporate crimes division," the inspector replied. "Most of the media is controlled by the major sponsors. They have done their best to paint him as a menace to the sport. The truth is he's our most valuable weapon against these villains."

Spritle poked his head back up. "Why does he always cover his face?" Racer X snapped a look toward him, and Spritle ducked away again. Chim-Chim squealed and did the same.

"If any of you knew my identity, you'd become targets for my enemies," Racer X replied coolly. "And those include some of the most vicious fixers."

"Fixers?" asked Speed's mother.

"Brutish thugs who intimidate drivers into losing on purpose," replied the inspector.

"What do you want with me?" asked Speed.

"Are you familiar with the driver Taejo Togokahn?" asked Inspector Detector.

"Of course," said Speed. He was a young up-and-coming driver just like Speed. Except Taejo had

the financial backing of his father's huge company, Togokahn Motors.

"For years he has been under the thumb of a fixer named Cruncher Block. And we know that Block works for Royalton," the inspector explained.

"Recently, Taejo has been forced to lose races that have led to a drop in the stock price of Togokahn Motors. We believe this is a part of a corporate strategy to allow Royalton Industries to buy control of Togokahn." He took another sip of his coffee. "Taejo doesn't want this to happen and he began resisting, thinking that he could do it on his own. After his last race, he realized he needed help."

"He's throwing races?" asked Pops. "Why help him?"

"Because he has a file with enough information to connect Block to Royalton," replied the inspector. "It could put both of them behind bars for life."

Racer X jumped in. "The problem is, he won't give us the file unless we help him stop the takeover of his family's company."

"How can you stop the takeover?" asked Speed.

"There is an upcoming race that Taejo believes he can win," the inspector replied. "If he does, it will catapult Togokahn Motors back into the spotlight and double the cost of the buyout. That alone should kill the takeover."

"But there aren't any more races left except for the Grand Prix," said Sparky. "Both Speed and

Taejo failed to qualify during Fuji."

"There aren't any track races," Racer X corrected. "But there's a cross-country rally."

"You mean, the Crucible?" asked Sparky.

"What?" asked Pops.

The Crucible was the nickname for the Casa Cristo Classic, the last race Rex ever drove.

"I know it seems cruel to ask, but Taejo made it clear that he had to have Speed and X on his team or there would be no deal," said the inspector.

Speed knew why Taejo was so desperate to win the Casa Cristo. The winner of the dangerous rally gets an automatic invitation to drive in the Grand Prix. And what better way to be in the spotlight than by racing in the world's greatest race!

Pops leaped to his feet. "Out of the question!"

"You'll have the support of the entire CIB," said Inspector Detector.

Pops shook his head. "No! Rally racing is a back-alley sport full of jackals, headhunters, and thugs! I'm sorry, Inspector, but I lost one son to that death trap. I won't lose another."

The inspector reached into his pocket and pulled out a business card. "I understand. If you change your mind . . ."

Pops waved it away. "Keep your card, Inspector."

Speed glanced over at Racer X. The masked racer simply stared at him through his dark mask. A chill ran down Speed's spine.

That night, Speed and Trixie drove back to Inspiration Point. It began to rain, so he extended the glass dome over the Mach 5's cockpit. Instead of gazing at the stars, they laid the seats back and watched the raindrops run down the clear shield. Speed filled Trixie in on everything that happened earlier that day. He told her that he was seriously considering the inspector's offer, even if it meant working with the notorious Racer X.

"After Fuji, I just don't know," Speed said. "I've got to do something."

"But Pops will never let you go," said Trixie.

He turned to her and smiled. "He won't if I *ask* him."

Trixie gasped. "Speed Racer, what are you thinking?"

"You weren't in Royalton's office, Trix," he explained. "You don't know what it was like. It felt as though he had his hand inside my chest. Like he was trying to crush everything in my life that matters to me."

Trixie crossed her arms. "I hate him. I'm picturing his heart clogging with cholesterol right now."

Speed laughed. "No joke, Trix. If you could have

been in that room, you'd want to do anything you could to take this guy down."

Trixie was quiet for a moment. Then she sat up. "All right. Let's do it. You're going to need an alibi. We'll say we're going skiing."

"We?" asked Speed. "No way!"

"You're going to need my help," she said. "Casa Cristo is a rally. I can spot from my 'copter."

"Trixie, this isn't a game," said Speed. "These people play rough."

"I know. That's why I'm coming with you." She gave a devious grin. "And if you even try to argue with me, I'll tell Pops right now and he won't let you out of his sight."

"You would, wouldn't you?" asked Speed.

Her grin widened as she nodded.

Speed turned on the car and put it in gear. "Well, I guess we're going skiing then."

Chapter 15

For once, everything seemed to be going as planned. Speed's parents bought their story, and he and Trixie went on their "ski trip." But before heading to Casa Cristo, Speed made a stop at the CIB design lab. Once inside, he was met by Inspector Detector. "Speed, I want you to understand how much the CIB appreciates your help on this."

"I'm not doing this to help the CIB," Speed replied. "I don't know anything about corporate crimes and honestly, if I did, it wouldn't really matter. I'm doing this because someone is trying to hurt my family and I'm going to do everything I can to hurt him back."

"Good," said a voice behind him. It was Racer X. He motioned for Speed to follow. "Then you're going to love this."

He followed the masked racer into a large automotive bay. The Mach 5 was perched on a lift and swarming with mechanics and technicians. Racer X didn't lead him to the car, though. Instead he brought Speed over to a slender woman sitting in front of a computer. She wore glasses and had her dark hair pulled away from her face.

"This is Minx," he said. "She builds my cars."

"Nice to meet you," said Speed. Minx nodded and resumed typing on the computer keyboard.

"Speed, you'll be racing against some of the most dangerous drivers in the world," said the inspector. "We expect they'll do anything they can to stop you."

Minx tapped a few more keys. A computer graphic of the Mach 5 appeared on the screen. "Their cars will probably be equipped with secret weapons," Minx announced. "So we've modified the Mach 5 to try to counter their attacks."

She pressed another key and a close-up of the Mach 5's steering wheel flew into view. In the center, six buttons surrounded a single large button. They were labeled A through G.

"The A button will operate your jump jacks," said Minx. She moved the cursor over the A button and four skids protruded from the undercarriage. They telescoped out on round metal legs.

She moved the cursor to the next button. A clear dome extended over the image of the car's two seats. "B will seal your cockpit," she explained. "We've fortified your dome with a bulletproof coating." Animated machine guns appeared and blasted the clear bubble. Their animated bullets ricocheted off the screen.

"Should someone go after your tires with, say, a hidden shank or a shredder," said Minx, "the C button will activate your tire shields." Metal discs fanned out from the Mach 5's tire rims. "However in

the event of any blowout, D will inflate a Hexa-Dyno emergency spare." One of the computer tires blew up only to be replaced with a new one.

Minx pointed to the E button. "E will activate these Zircon-lipped saw blades." Two huge circular saws shot out of the car's nose. Attached to long robotic arms, they spun as the arms slashed them back and forth. "They'll cut through almost anything. Use with discretion."

Minx tapped a few more keys, and the screen was filled with a close-up of a tire. "F will project the tire crampons," said Minx. Several spikes erupted from the tire's tread. Slightly curved, they would make easy work of any slick terrain.

The full Mach 5 appeared again as Minx pointed to the G button. "And finally G will launch a remote-control homing bird. It's capable of transmitting video footage right to your cockpit." Speed watched as a hatch slid open on the hood and a birdlike robot appeared. It rose above the car and flew away, the compartment closing behind it.

"This is going to be an interesting race," said Trixie.

Once Speed was satisfied with the Mach 5's modifications, he, Trixie, and Racer X went to the whitewashed city of Casa Cristo. Their first stop was to meet Taejo Togokahn. They gathered in his luxury suite at the hotel along with his bodyguards and sister, Horuko.

Once everyone had been introduced, Taejo gave Speed a long bow. "It is an extraordinary honor to have such talent on my team."

"Let's skip the niceties and cut to the chase," said Racer X. "The only reason we're here is because you needed outside help. And because the inspector believes you'll turn over your file on Royalton and Cruncher Block."

Taejo smiled. "This is true."

"I don't believe it," said Racer X. "But I'm willing to take a chance that you'll prove me wrong."

"You won't regret your decision," said Taejo.

"We'll see," said Racer X. "Until then you have my word that I will do everything to make sure you checker at Brandenburg."

After leaving the hotel, Speed and Trixie had one more stop to make. They stood on the edge of town, on what would be the starting line for the race. Carved into natural stone was a huge memorial. Several bronze plaques covered the rock. Above them, huge letters were carved: IN MEMORY OF THOSE WHO GAVE EVERYTHING FOR THEIR LOVE OF THIS SPORT.

Speed knelt and ran his fingers over the letters on one particular plaque. The letters spelled out REX RACER. Trixie gently placed a hand upon his back.

"I understand it now, Trix," said Speed. "I know why he left us." His throat tightened as tears formed in his eyes. "He was trying to change this rotten business and they killed him for it."

Chapter 16

Cruncher Block only had a couple of loose ends to tie before the Casa Cristo race began. Royalton hadn't been at all pleased when Cruncher informed him that Team Togokahn had entered at the last minute. He was absolutely furious when he heard who Taejo's teammates were. Royalton had given the fixer unlimited resources to make sure Taejo, Speed, and Racer X didn't finish the race. Cruncher already had the Yen-Che team in his pocket. They were quite ruthless and usually got the job done. However, he had to increase his insurance by visiting a few other competing teams.

First he saw Delila, the team leader of Flying Foxes Freight. He caught up to the redhead as she was charming a deadly cobra with a flute. He gave her a velvet bag of jewels in exchange for her team taking out Team Togokahn.

Next he paid a visit to the longhouse of the Vikings team. They drove for Thor-axine Inc. As the leader bit into a huge turkey leg, Cruncher had his boys place a huge trunk onto the Vikings' long dinner table. The Vikings opened it to reveal it stuffed full of the finest animal pelts. The Vikings were in.

Then he went to the underground bunker of

the Sempre Fi-ber team. There was only one thing that could bribe that group of military wannabes: a briefcase full of cold hard cash.

Now, he had two more items on his pre-race checklist. The first was dealing with Snake Oiler. He was a particularly unscrupulous racer on the Hydra-Cell team.

"But this is supposed to be my race!" Snake whined when Cruncher told him all about Team Togokahn entering the race. "I'm supposed to win! I got the green light! They promised I'd get to go to the Grand Prix! For eight years I've played by the rules! This is supposed to be *my* race!"

Cruncher put his big hands to the side of his head. "Enough!" he roared. "I can't stand the whining!"

Cruncher leaned in close to Snake's face. "It's simple. We have a team of wild cards." He poked a finger onto the whiner's chest. "The problem is that these wild cards are better drivers than you."

Snake backed away. "The heck they are!"

"Prove it," Cruncher challenged. "Take out Taejo. The other two will quit."

"You just watch me!" Snake stormed out of Cruncher's hotel room.

Cruncher sighed. Now he had just one more thing to do to ensure that Team Togokahn didn't win. He went to the bureau and picked up a fish bowl. One of his *babies*, a small, deadly piranha,

slowly circled the tiny bowl. Its sharp teeth rose and fell as it opened and closed its large mouth. Cruncher placed the bowl in a cushioned box and closed the lid. He handed it to one of his men.

"Take this to the front desk," Cruncher instructed. "Tell them to deliver it to Horuko Togokahn."

"You got it, boss," said the thug. With a hint of fright, he carefully carried the box out of the hotel room.

Although Cruncher sent the package to Taejo's sister, the message was for Taejo himself. Throw the race, or his sister gets to meet *all* of Cruncher's little babies.

The morning sky had just begun to brighten as the Casa Cristo racers climbed into their cars. Speed ran a systems check on the Mach 5, making sure everything was operational. Taejo had men guarding the cars all night so he was fairly certain nothing had been tampered with. However, it never hurt to be thorough.

Once Speed was satisfied, he pulled on his helmet and climbed into the cockpit. He strapped on his harness and started the car. The familiar roar and vibration of the engine filled his senses. He even wore his lucky red socks. Speed Racer was as ready as he was ever going to be.

He pulled to the starting line along with Taejo and Racer X. Speed and the masked racer flanked their team leader. It was going to be a different race for Speed. For the first time, he wasn't trying to win. His job was to make sure Taejo won—and that he came out of it in one piece.

The beginning of the track ran parallel to a cliff's edge, overlooking the ocean. On the other side of the track, crowds of people packed onto stone bleachers. They cheered as the drivers all started their engines. As the sky grew brighter, the racers revved their engines. It sounded like thunder before a storm.

Wearing a colorful, layered sarong, the Queen of Casa Cristo strolled onto the ramparts overlooking the stands. The race officially began with the rising sun. And as the sun poked over the horizon, she raised a flare pistol above her head and fired it.

The race was on!

Speed hit the gas as the column of cars began to move. Sand and gravel ricocheted off his windshield as tires spun out around him. The spectators cheered as the cars pulled away. Sparks flew as drivers immediately began nudging one another. Each tried to make their way to the front of the pack.

The first major obstacle was the Muqranna. Sprawled out like an ancient obstacle course, it was a honeycomb of stone columns and archways. As

the cars jockeyed for position early in the race, the danger-level rose. The battle at the front of the pack resulted in a small pileup as the first few drivers began weaving through the stone forest. As cars crashed, fireballs filled Speed's view and he had to swerve to miss the flaming debris. It was difficult enough slaloming through the Muqranna. Dodging other drivers doing the same and missing flying debris tripled the difficulty level.

As the drivers left the arches, the racers funneled onto a cliff-side road. It slowly wound and climbed away from the coast and into the nearby mountains. Along the way, Speed and his teammates made quick work of passing other drivers. With swift precision, they slowly made their way to the front of the pack.

Trixie's voice sounded in Speed's headset. She was flying above the race in her helicopter. "Speed, watch the Yen-Che team! They just dropped back. I think they're up to something." Speed knew Trixie had her hands full not only watching the race but dodging the other spotting 'copters. Not to mention the news blimps.

"Thanks, Trix," he replied.

Speed let off the gas, drifting closer to Taejo. Racer X did the same. After all, they had to keep Taejo safe. Then Speed checked the rearview mirror and saw the Yen-Che team closing in. The harsh angles of their currency-clad cars were hard to miss.

Suddenly, one of the tires blew out on the lead Yen-Che car. The explosion forced it into a spin, flinging it right toward the Mach 5. The jagged car came at him like a Japanese throwing star.

Speed pressed the A button, activating the jump jacks. His car sprung clear of the Yen-Che car and landed safely back on the road.

Meanwhile, Racer X moved in, slamming his car against the spinning Yen-Che car. The force of the impact launched the Yen-Che driver through the guardrail and over the cliff.

Speed intercepted another Yen-Che car. He slammed into its side, sending it careening out of control. It smashed through a billboard and out of the race as well.

The last attacking car barreled straight for Taejo. Racer X swerved behind it, slamming his front bumper into the enemy's rear bumper. He activated jacks of his own, popping up only the front of his car. The bump caused the Yen-Che to be tossed end-over-end like a pancake. Racer X drove under the flipping car just before it smashed to the ground, upside down. The entire Yen-Che team had been swiftly dealt with.

Speed shifted into a higher gear as he and his teammates poured on the speed. They followed the road as it wound away from the cliffs and through a large valley. Huge mountain peaks jutted up on both sides of the road. Soon, the thin road led to an open desert flat. They had officially left the mountains and entered the Zunubian Desert. Now they could spread out a bit.

"Come on!" yelled Taejo. "We're falling behind!"

Trixie broke in. "Speed! On your left! The Flying Foxes!"

He glanced left to see three pink cars in tight formation. "Got 'em!" Speed acknowledged. The lead car pulled alongside the Mach 5. It was Delila, the leader of the Flying Foxes. She winked and gave Speed a devious smile.

"They're not alone," added Racer X.

Three military-styled vehicles closed in on their right. The large cars were covered in camouflage paint and driven by mean-looking guys. It was the Sempre Fi-ber team.

"Check your rearview," said Taejo.

Speed glanced at his mirror to see a terrifying sight. Rumbling up from behind were three souped-up Viking war wagons. Each of the drivers had long horns jutting out from the sides of their helmets. It was the Thor-axine Inc. team.

As the enemy teams closed in, it was clear that none of them cared about winning the race. They were all there to take out Speed Racer and his teammates.

Chapter 17

The Flying Foxes were the next to strike. As Delila moved in, tire shanks jutted from her hubcaps. She slammed into the side of the Mach 5, shredding two of Speed's tires. His car spun wildly out of control. His body pulled at the restraints as the world outside the cockpit became a blur.

Instinctively, he hit the jacks. They erupted from the car, causing it to flip into the air. While he was upside down, Speed hit the D button. His Hexa-Dyno spares inflated in place of the shredded tires. When he hit the ground, he landed on four good tires.

Now far behind his team, Speed hit the gas. As he closed in, he saw Delila to the left of Taejo. This time he was ready. Speed activated the tire shields and slid himself in between her and Taejo. Taejo pulled away as Speed and Delila scraped against each other. He held the wheel tightly as she tried to shove him off the road.

"Speed! Look right!" shouted Trixie.

Speed turned in time to see another Flying Fox moving in fast. Speed slammed on the brakes. He shot backward as the Fox on the right slammed into Delila's car. Her blades inadvertently slashed her teammate's tires. The second car spun out of control and out of the race.

"Okay," said Speed. "No more Mr. Nice Guy."

He pulled closer to Delila's car and pressed the E button on his steering wheel. Two saw blades erupted from the nose of the Mach 5. Speed reached down and toggled a joystick on the center console. He used it to position the whirling blades vertically. As he hit the accelerator, the blades ran down the side of Delila's car. They sliced away her tire shanks. He retracted the blades and slammed into her rear bumper, sending her spinning out of the way. Now that Delila was taken care of, Speed shoved the gas pedal to the floor, heading back to his teammates.

Taejo sped across the desert as Racer X did his best to fend off the Thor-axine and Sempre Fi-ber teams. As the Mach 5 barreled toward them, one of the Viking cars zeroed-in on Taejo. Speed slid into the thick of things, taking the blow for Taejo.

"Where have you been?" asked Taejo.

"Have any of these drivers read the rule book?" asked Speed.

In retaliation, the Thor-axine driver activated jump jacks of his own. His car leaped sideways, over the Mach 5. When he was directly overhead, a huge Norse hammer swung from beneath the wagon's undercarriage. Speed ducked as the weapon swung through his open cockpit.

"See?" asked Speed. "This race is full of cheaters!"

Taejo laughed as he dodged a Sempre Fi-ber attack. "First rule of rally racing: If you aren't cheating, you aren't trying."

"Heads-up!" warned Racer X. "Here they come again!"

As Speed and Racer X fended off the enemy cars, they stirred up a hurricane of dirt and sand. They lured attacking cars away from Taejo, rammed them into sand dunes, and spun them out of the race. No matter what secret weapons the attacking drivers employed, Speed and Racer X were ready for them. The two worked together so well that if Speed didn't know any better, he would have believed he and the masked racer had been driving together for years.

"Lead him," said Racer X.

Just as Racer X suggested, Speed herded one of the Sempre Fi-bers to the other side of Taejo's car, where Racer X was waiting. "Here you go!" said Speed.

The masked racer flipped the Sempre Fi-ber car into the air and out of the race.

Speed and Racer X were the perfect team. It was almost as if Speed could predict every move that Racer X was going to make.

"Wing left," said Racer X.

"Flying in!" said Speed. He jumped Taejo's car and blocked an attack on Racer X.

A Thor-axine car jacked into the air. It arced

above the others, heading straight for Taejo. It was about to squash him like a bug.

"Taejo!" yelled Trixie.

"All yours, Speed," said Racer X.

Speed cut his wheels and pulled the hand brake. While the Mach 5 went into a spin, he hit the jacks. The race car flew into the air after the Viking car. As if delivering a flying karate kick, the Mach 5 knocked the Thor-axine car away from Taejo. As Speed landed on all four wheels, the enemy car tumbled across the desert flats. It smashed into a dune and exploded. Lucky for the Viking, his kwik-save cocoon popped out of the flames and bounced across the desert.

Speed and Racer X slowly finished off most of the attacking cars as they barreled through the desert. They took out a few more as they drove past the aqueducts of Sassicaia. By the time they reached Cortega, the town at the end of the first leg of the rally, all the attacking vehicles had been dispatched. But unfortunately, Taejo's team was not in the lead. Snake Oiler and his Hydra-Cell team were first to finish that day's leg of the race.

When they pulled into the Togokahn hangar, Taejo was furious. "If we drive like that tomorrow we will lose!" He pointed at Racer X. "You will get nothing! All of this will be meaningless!"

"Relax!" said Speed. "Snake is weak on turns. We'll catch him in the mountains."

"We might if you stop showing off!" accused Taejo.

Furious, Speed lurched forward. "Hey, all I was doing was saving your butt!"

Taejo raised a fist, but Racer X caught it. "Don't fall apart yet. There's still a lot of race to run."

Taejo jerked free and stormed toward the exit. He was immediately enveloped by his security team.

"CIB men will be posted outside your hotel rooms," Racer X told Speed. "We made quite a statement today during the race. You and Trixie should be very careful tonight."

Speed stared at Racer X. He tried to imagine what he looked like under the mask. They both drove so well together, like they were taught by the same person. Was there a chance that Racer X was his brother? After all, Speed had hoped all along that Rex had somehow survived that deadly crash.

The masked racer turned to leave. "Racer X," said Speed. "I thought we made a good team today, it felt like . . . like we'd been doing it for a long time."

Racer X stared back for a moment. Finally, he shrugged and walked away. "If you say so."

That night at the hotel, Speed and Trixie ordered room service. Even though he'd barely had any food all day, Speed was too excited to eat. "It

was very weird, Trix," he said. "I knew every move he was going to make and he knew mine. It was so familiar. Maybe I'm crazy, but Racer X first showed up two years after Rex's death."

"But, Speed, Rex was cremated," said Trixie.

"A *body* was cremated," said Speed. "It had been badly burned in the crash, so even if it was really Rex, no one could have recognized him."

Trixie's mouth tightened. "So you think he faked the crash with a different body in the driver's seat?"

Speed shrugged. "Somehow the kwik-save was disconnected. Inspector Detector suspected foul play but nothing could be proved."

"Do you really think Rex could put everyone through all that?" she asked.

Speed pushed the food around on his plate. "Maybe he felt he didn't have any other choice."

There was a knock at the door.

Speed sprang to his feet. After all the attacks during the race today, he was still paranoid that someone was out to get him. He opened the door just a crack. It was one of the CIB men. "I'm sorry to disturb you, sir, but do you know these people?"

Speed looked past him to see Sprible, Chim-Chim, Sparky, and a very angry Mom and Pops.

Chapter 18

Speed sat on the edge of the bed while Pops paced about the room. "Is this the kind of driver I have? Someone who disobeys? Someone who lies to me?" he asked. "Is this the kind of son I've raised?" He shook his head. "You know what this race did to this family. Did you stop to think about us? Huh? Did you think about your mother? Or Sprtile? What it would do to them if something happened to you?"

"That's all I *have* been thinking about, Pops," Speed replied. "You, Mom, Spritle, Sparky."

Chim-Chim screeched. He and Spritle were picking through Speed and Trixie's unfinished dinner. A spaghetti noodle hung from the chimp's lips.

Speed smiled. "Yeah, you too, Chim-Chim." He turned back to his father. "We're in serious trouble, Pops, and it's all my fault."

"This is not the place or the race to do anything about that," said Pops.

"Why not?" asked Speed.

"Because it won't do any good!"

Speed got to his feet. "You don't know that!"

"You think you can drive a car and change the world?" asked Pops. "It doesn't work like that!"

"Maybe not," replied Speed. "But it's the only thing I know how to do. And I've got to do something."

 **83**

"That's unacceptable!" bellowed Pops. He motioned to Trixie. "This is over. Both of you, pack your things. We're going home."

Speed shook his head. "I can't. I'm staying."

Trixie nodded. "So am I."

"I'm not a child, Pops," said Speed. "You can't tell me how to live my life. If you want to fire me as your driver, then fine, do it. But it won't change the fact that I'm going to finish this race."

Pops moved in on Speed. "You sound just like Rex! Do you want to die like him, too?"

Speed shot back. "Don't take it out on me because you feel guilty for what happened to Rex!"

Speed's mother pushed between them. "Okay, you two. That's enough. Pops, if they're staying, then we're staying."

"All right!" yelled Spritle. "Room service!"

"I suggest we try to do everything we can to make sure we go home together," said Mom.

For a moment it didn't look as if Pops would listen. His eyes narrowed at Speed. "All right," he said through clenched teeth. "Where's the Mach 5?"

Speed took a deep breath. "With security."

"You added something to it?" asked Pops.

"Some defensive modifications," said Speed.

Pops nodded his head. "The whole thing is out of balance, isn't it, Speed?"

Speed relaxed. "It pulls left. Rides a little stiff."

Pops sighed, turned, and marched for the door.

"Sparky!" he barked. The young mechanic flashed Speed a smile and then followed Pops to where the Mach 5 was being held.

Speed plopped down on the bed. "I'm sorry, Mom."

"Your father loves you," she said. "He's just afraid that . . ."

"I know," said Speed. "But it's going to be okay."

"You wouldn't lie to me, would you?" she asked.

Speed smiled. "Never again."

That night, Speed's mom stayed with Trixie in the adjoining hotel room. Everyone else crashed with Speed. Pops, Sparky, Spritle, and Chim-Chim were scattered around the room on cots and couches. Luckily, Speed didn't have to share his bed with anyone. He needed all the rest he could get before the final leg of the race.

Unfortunately, Speed was startled from his sleep by Spritle's loud scream. Speed's eyes sprung open to see a ninja standing right over him. The black-clad assassin aimed a hypodermic syringe at Speed's neck. Speed caught the ninja's hand just as he was about to jab the needle into him. Speed and the ninja grappled with each other, but Speed managed to get the upper hand. Speed forced the ninja's hand away from his neck and guided the syringe into the headboard.

From out of the darkness, Sparky leaped onto the ninja's back. "I got him!" he yelled. But the ninja threw the young mechanic across the room.

Speed got to his feet and threw a quick combo. He connected with two punches, but the ninja blocked the third. Then the assassin did a spin kick that knocked Speed back onto the bed.

Speed switched on the light just in time to see the ninja make a break for the open window. Before he escaped, Spritle and Chim-Chim latched onto the ninja's legs. Confused and off balance, the assassin stumbled over an ottoman.

"You attack my family?!" boomed Pops Racer. "You try to hurt my son?!"

Spritle and Chim-Chim backed away as Pops stomped toward the ninja. The masked man tried to scramble away, but Pops's large hands clamped down on him. He twisted and spun the squirming ninja in a series of wrestling moves. He put him in a headlock and slammed him to the ground. Finally, Pops lifted the dizzy assassin high over his head and tossed him out the window.

Hearing the commotion, Trixie and Speed's mother burst in from the adjoining room. "Was that a ninja?" asked Trixie.

"More like a *non*-ja," Pops replied. "Terrible what passes for a ninja these days."

Trixie smiled at Speed. "Cool beans."

Just then, there was a knock at Speed's door.

"I'll get it," said Pops cautiously.

Pops stumbled over the room wreckage as he made his way to the door. When Pops opened it, Speed heard a familiar voice speaking.

"Oh, I am sorry," said Taejo's sister, Horuko. "I was looking for Speed Racer."

Speed joined his father. "Horuko, are you okay?"

"No," she replied. "Something terrible has happened."

Everyone got dressed and met in Taejo's room. Several of his security guards were there along with the masked Racer X. Taejo lay in bed, hardly able to move. Horuko explained how someone had broken into his room earlier that night.

Racer X examined a small blow dart. He pressed the tip lightly to his tongue. "Narcolyte Benzamine," he said. "A highly effective and debilitating drug. Stays in the system for hours, but leaves no trace."

"I'll be fine by morning," slurred Taejo.

"No, you won't," said Racer X. "You can't drive a car. You can barely stand up."

"Don't tell me what I can do." Taejo struggled to his feet, but instead crumpled to the ground.

"Taejo!" yelled Horuko. She knelt beside him and cradled his head. Her brother was out cold.

Speed couldn't believe it. Without Taejo in the race, Team Togokahn would have to forfeit. "What are we going to do?"

Trixie stepped forward. "I have an idea."

Chapter 19

The next morning, without the Flying Foxes, Sempre Fi-ber and Thor-axine teams, there were considerably less racers pulling out of Cortega. Cheering crowds lined the cobblestone streets as the racers roared by. The cars already began to nudge and buck, jockeying for position in the early morning light.

As before, Speed and Racer X took up positions on either side of Taejo's car. Unfortunately, Speed was far more nervous today than he was yesterday.

Another race car drifted dangerously close to Taejo's car. "Watch your line!" ordered Speed.

Taejo's car accelerated, dodging the opposing car. Unfortunately, it overshot them on a turn and caused Racer X to drift toward Speed. Sparks flew as X's car scraped metal with the Mach 5.

"Watch it!" shouted Speed.

"Calm down," said Racer X. "It will be fine."

Pops and Sparky rode in Trixie's helicopter. "The pack is leaning left," said Sparky. "Look for a slingshot on your right!"

As they left the city, the Togokahn team soared up the right side of the pack. As they closed in on Snake Oiler and the Hydra-Cell team, another car drifted in, trying to block them. Racer X jumped

over the car while Taejo's car sped past.

"Speed, you're too tight!" shouted Racer X.

The enemy car smacked the rear of the Mach 5, sending it spinning. Speed growled in frustration as he jerked the wheel and hit the gas. He pulled out of the spin and roared back toward his team. "This is completely . . ."

". . . absolutely crazy," finished Pops from the helicopter.

Sparky continued to spot for them as they headed up a mountain pass. "Wicked sidewinder coming up," he said. "Watch the inside-out. Could get ugly."

The congested pack of race cars roared up the steep road as it turned back and forth up the mountain. All along the road, cars bumped off one another like they were balls in a pinball machine. A car got past Speed and bumped into Taejo's car. Taejo's car accelerated to escape, but was going too fast to make the next turn.

"Left!" ordered Speed. "Drift tight! Tight!" Taejo's wheels locked as it skidded for the edge of the cliff. "No!" yelled Speed.

Meanwhile Cruncher Block sat, waiting, in the pilot's seat of the Togokahn luxury helicopter. The real pilot was bound and gagged inside a storage compartment. Since all his hired driving teams failed to stop the Taejo team, Cruncher had to take matters into his own hands. He had warned Taejo

that something terrible would happen to his sister if he didn't throw the race. Now Cruncher was going to follow through on his threat. His only regret was that he didn't have his piranhas with him.

When Horuko and her bodyguards boarded their helicopter, they didn't even take a glance at their pilot. This was too easy! Once the passengers were seated, Cruncher simply lifted the helicopter into the air and guided the craft away from Cortega. Cruncher gained altitude and headed for the mountains. He pulled the helicopter into the clouds, out of view of the other flying craft in the area.

Cruncher set the autopilot and moved back toward the rear cabin. Before opening the door, he drew his pistol. As he stepped inside, the two bodyguards reached for their weapons.

"Don't do it!" shouted Cruncher. The men slowly raised their hands. "On the ground!" he ordered.

As the men sank to the floor, Cruncher turned to Taejo's sister. She wore a dark cloak with a hood obscuring her face. Cruncher lifted the hood. "Gotcha," he said.

"What the . . ." muttered Cruncher as the hood fell away. Horuko wasn't looking back at him. It was Taejo. The poison had worn off! The man smiled as he swatted the pistol from Cruncher's hand. The bodyguards got to their feet and drew their guns.

"But if you're here," said Cruncher, "who's driving your car?"

Chapter 20

Taejo's car pulled out of the skid at the last minute. The back tires spun gravel as it zoomed back onto the road. As they continued up the mountain, Speed pulled up beside Taejo's car.

"That's better," said Trixie as she removed her helmet and shook out her hair. "I couldn't see."

"Nice save, Trix," said Sparky. "Top of the hill's coming. Snake's got a quarter of a mile on you."

"Well, let's go get him," said Trixie.

"If you'd be a little more careful, he wouldn't be ahead of us," scolded Speed.

"I told you I couldn't see out of this dang helmet," said Trixie. "It's too big."

Speed sighed. "I can't believe you talked us into this ridiculous idea."

"What's ridiculous about it?" asked Trixie. "You're the one always telling me I'm a better driver than most of the drivers in the WRL." She pulled ahead of Speed.

Speed zoomed by. "Now's not the time to prove it!"

"Why not?" asked Trixie. She darted back ahead, cutting him off.

Speed tried to pass again. "It's too dangerous!"

Trixie swerved to block him. "Too dangerous for me but not for you?"

"Children, focus!" barked Racer X. "If we're going to have a chance, we're going to have to pass Snake before the rendezvous."

Trixie pulled away fast. "I'm ready. Let's roll."

"Wahoo!" yelled Sparky. "Go get 'em, girl!"

With Trixie between them, the Togokahn team made their way up the pack. This time, Speed and X went on the offensive. Racer X corner-checked opposing cars, clearing a path for Trixie. Meanwhile, Speed brought up the rear, fending off any retaliation. Every winding turn brought them closer to the leaders—the Hydra-Cell team.

After punching through the horde of race cars, there was finally no one between them and Snake Oiler. They climbed higher into the mountains, closing the gap. The cars dipped and rose as if sailing down a concrete river. Accelerating into the curves, they drifted through every turn. Soon, they were right on Snake Oiler's tail.

"Take them," said Racer X.

Speed smiled. "With pleasure."

In a slingshot maneuver, the Mach 5 shot past Trixie and Racer X. Soon he was right alongside the Hydra-Cell team. Snake's car screeched to the side, blocking Speed's pass. Racer X zoomed through the gap and into the fray.

The Hydra-Cell team fought viciously to keep the lead. The gloves were off as they slammed into the Togokahn cars. They tried to run them off the

road and down the side of the mountain. Fortunately, they couldn't land a solid blow. Racer X wedged one of the Hydra-Cell's cars into a rock wall. It bounced off and spun out behind them.

Trixie pulled ahead of another car and cut it off. The car fishtailed and almost broke through the guardrail. It skidded to a stop to keep from plummeting down the mountainside.

"Oh yeah!" yelled Sparky.

Speed went after Snake himself. He rammed and battered his car so much, Snake began to flinch with Speed's every move. Finally, Speed floored it and zipped past him. At the last second, Speed slapped his back bumper against the corner of Snake's nose. Snake's car spun out behind Speed.

"That's my boy," said Pops from above.

Trixie and Racer X swerved around Snake as they joined Speed. Their team was finally in the lead.

Soon small snowbanks appeared on the roadside as they climbed higher into the mountain range. Speed Racer and his teammates drove as fast as they safely could through the hairpin turns. They had to put as much distance between them and the other racers if their plan was going to work.

When they reached the secret rendezvous point, they turned onto an unpaved road that opened onto a wide, wooded plateau. Trixie's helicopter was parked next to the Togokahn helicopter. Pops, Sparky, Taejo, Horuko, and her bodyguards stood waiting.

Horuko glanced around nervously. "Are you sure there are no cameras here?"

"I checked it out this morning," Pops replied. "Quite a few dead spots in these mountains." He and Sparky went to work refueling the cars.

Speed leaped out of the Mach 5 and marched over to Trixie. "I told you . . ." he began. She tensed, ready for a fight. But then Speed smiled. ". . . you're one hell of a driver."

Trixie smiled. "You're not so bad yourself."

"What's he doing here?" asked Racer X.

Speed followed his gaze to see the notorious Cruncher Block strapped to a seat in Horuko's helicopter.

"Stowaway," said Taejo. "Weren't sure what to do with him."

Racer X crossed his arms. "Do what he'd do to us," he said. "Break his legs and let him walk back."

Taejo removed his cloak and revealed his racing jumpsuit underneath. Trixie gave him his helmet and he climbed into his car.

Horuko bowed to Trixie, "Thank you so much."

Trixie laughed. "It was a blast."

"The cars are refueled!" announced Sparky.

Speed hopped into the Mach 5. "Let's go!"

Suddenly, the sound of gunfire filled the air. Men with machine guns stepped out of the woods.

"Nobody move!" one of the shooters shouted.

Chapter 21

"What is this?" asked Pops. He stepped forward, but a stream of bullets churned up the earth and snow at his feet. Pops halted.

One of the men untied Cruncher. "This is called a change of plan," said Cruncher.

"Yeah, that's right," agreed one of his thugs. "We're changing your plan that changed our plan to change your plan. Right, boss?"

Cruncher rolled his eyes. Then he grinned as he strode toward Racer X. "The new plan . . . what was it, again?" he glanced down. "Oh, yeah! Break your legs and make you walk back? I like that."

He motioned for two of his men. They swooped in behind Racer X and grabbed his arms. "But first, I think it's time to play a little peekaboo, I-see-you," said Cruncher.

Racer X struggled but it was no good. The men held him tightly as their boss reached for his mask.

Just then, a rock flew past Speed's head and struck Cruncher smack between the eyes. Cruncher grabbed his face. "Ow!"

"Yes!" yelled a familiar voice. Speed turned to see Spritle and Chim-Chim poking out of the Mach 5's trunk. Spritle held his slingshot as he and the chimp exchanged a high five.

"Spritle?" asked Pops.

"Get them!" shouted Cruncher.

With everyone's attention on Spritle, Racer X broke free from the men holding him. Speed kicked the gun from the nearest thug while Trixie gave a karate chop to the goon next to her. Taejo jumped into the fray along with Pops and Sparky. Soon, the entire plateau was covered in a giant brawl.

Speed and Trixie took down two of the men while Pops held another thug in a headlock. That left Racer X the chance to go toe-to-toe with Cruncher Block. Racer X knocked the large thug through the air. Cruncher slid across the snow, coming to a stop in front of a fallen machine gun. As Cruncher reached for it, Taejo's foot came down on his hand.

"Looks like another change of plans," said Racer X.

The fight was over quickly with Cruncher's men looking the worse for the wear. Horuko's bodyguards picked up their guns and herded the goons into a tight group.

"Spritle!" yelled Pops. "Get over here!"

Spritle and Chim-Chim hid behind Speed.

Speed turned and knelt beside the youngsters. "This isn't a game, you guys. You could've been killed stowing away in the trunk."

Spritle and Chim-Chim hung their heads. "I know it was bad," said Spritle. "I know we shouldn't

96

have done it." He leaned forward and whispered. "And Chim-Chim was really, really scared."

The chimp shot him a look.

"Chim-Chim?" asked Speed.

Spritle smiled. "Okay, I was a little scared, too." He threw his arms around Speed. "I didn't want what happened to Rex to happen to you." Speed laughed as Chim-Chim joined the hug. "We just thought if you got into trouble, maybe we could help," Spritle added. "And it's a good thing we did."

Speed gave a pleading look to Pops. His father shook his head. He marched forward. "Oh, no, you're not getting off that easy." He grabbed Spritle and Chim-Chim by the scruffs of their necks. "If your mother hasn't had a heart attack already, I'm sure she'll know what to do with you two."

Suddenly, the sound of engines filled the air. Speed ran to the edge of the plateau. The Hydra-Cell team sped by on the road below.

Taejo ran to his car. "Go! Go! Go!"

Speed and Racer X hopped into their cars as well. Engines growled, tires spun, and gravel spit across the road as the three drivers shot back into the race.

While Horuko and her bodyguards took off in their own helicopter, the others boarded Trixie's helicopter. Speed would need their help spotting trouble from above.

Chapter 22

Speed and the others drove as fast as they could to catch up to Snake Oiler and his teammates. With every turn, Speed hoped to see the cars ahead of them. Unfortunately, with every turn, he was disappointed.

As they tore down the winding mountain highway, the snowbanks appeared more frequently and with more volume. They had to slow down on the turns for fear of hitting ice patches and flying off the mountain. Speed's chest tightened the deeper they drove into the frozen landscape. He knew what was up ahead—the Maltese Ice Caves.

The caves were where the highway went straight through a giant glacier. As the enormous carpet of ice slowly moved through the valley, new tunnels had to be built to keep the road open. This left frozen catacombs where light reflected and refracted from every direction. It would probably be the most dangerous terrain on which Speed would ever race. But that wasn't why he was apprehensive. His brother, Rex Racer, had lost his life in those very caverns.

Speed hoped that they would overtake the Hydra-Cell team before reaching the caves. But no such luck. As they rounded the final turn through

the mountains, he saw Snake's team disappear inside the giant glacier.

Speed gripped the wheel as his team soared toward the narrow entrance. Speed was so consumed by the thought of Rex's death, that he floored the accelerator without even realizing it.

"Speed? What are you doing?" shouted Taejo.

"Sorry," he said. He let off the gas, falling to the back of the line.

The sky disappeared as they entered the glass-like tunnel. Warped reflections of their cars kept pace as they slalomed through huge columns of ice. Speed could feel the tires skid a bit as he passed over patches of ice on the road. He tried his best to put Rex out of his mind. He had to concentrate on driving.

"Are you all right?" asked Racer X.

"I'm fine," said Speed.

"The next cave's a rattler," said Racer X.

"What's that?" asked Taejo.

Speed sighed. "A double S."

"We'll make our move in there," said Racer X.

They caught up to the enemy team just as they entered the rattler. The thin cave opened up into a huge cavern. Although it made two very sharp S curves, there was plenty of room to maneuver and pass. It was also the last cavern in the glacier.

"Now," said Racer X.

The three of them broke formation, spreading

wide. Taejo and Racer X grappled with cars on the outside while Speed sped by them. He aimed straight for the lead car, Snake Oiler.

Thankfully, the ensuing battle took Speed's mind off his brother. It was difficult enough sparring with another race car while driving over a hundred miles per hour. It was three times as hard doing so in an ice cave. Speed had to overcompensate on every move. The rear wheels of the Mach 5 often seemed as if they had minds of their own. He fishtailed around the turns before slamming back into Snake's car.

Behind him, Taejo and Racer X were having better luck. One by one, they took out the enemy cars. One competitor's car spun like a top as it disappeared down a side tunnel. The other ran off the road and embedded itself into a wall of ice. That just left Speed and Snake Oiler.

Luckily, there was light at the end of the tunnel—literally. Up ahead, a blue circle marked the end of the ice caves. If Speed couldn't take out Snake inside the glacier, he could do it back on solid pavement.

The two cars continued to careen into each other as they neared the exit. Then, at the last moment, Snake pulled ahead. Speed hit the gas, ready to ram him from behind. Just then a white spray burst from Snake's rear bumper. It sprayed the road behind it. As the Mach 5 drove onto the substance,

it was immediately clear what Snake had done. The substance was freezing gas. Now the entire surface of the road was slick with ice.

The Mach 5 skidded as it neared the tunnel exit. Speed tried to compensate, but there was no use. He had no control at all. Ahead, Snake left the tunnel and followed the road to the right. His car continued to freeze the road behind him. Speed cut the wheels but he continued his slow spin. When he shot from the tunnel, he was completely turned around. The brakes were no good as he crashed through the guardrail and sailed off the side of the glacier.

"Speed!" yelled Racer X.

Speed expected to plummet through the air before smashing to the jagged rocks below. However, the car jolted as its tires hit the side of the glacier. Instead of tumbling down the mountain, the Mach 5 slid down the steep ice.

Speed immediately pressed the F button on his steering wheel. The car shook as the crampons jutted from his tire treads. Immediately he felt the difference, his descent slowed considerably. He hit another button and his front jacks fired, throwing the car into a somersault. Now that Speed was facing the right way, he could begin the drive back up the steep slope.

When the Mach 5 reached the top, Speed shot back onto the mountain road. He retracted the crampons and sped after Snake Oiler.

"Go, Speed, go!" shouted Sprisle.

"Sprisle, get off the radio," barked Pops.

Speed hugged every curve until he caught up to Taejo and Racer X. He zipped past them and barreled toward Snake Oiler. "Hi," Speed said as he bumped Snake's rear bumper. "Remember me?"

The freezing white gas erupted from Snake's car again but this time Speed was ready. The Mach 5 left skid marks on Snake's hood as he drove over him and into the lead.

The TV blimps overhead had their cameras trained on the action. Watching Speed Racer, one commentator exclaimed, "This kid is unbelievable!" Another commentator saw Snake Oiler make a sudden move. "Oh my," he shouted. "He's got a gun!"

Suddenly, Sparky's voice blared in Speed's headset. "Watch out Speed, he's got a gun!"

Speed checked his rearview mirror and saw Snake leaning out of his car, wielding a pistol. He activated the cockpit bubble a fraction of a second before bullets ricocheted off the coated glass. Not knowing how many hits the bubble would take, Speed jerked the wheel. The Mach 5 dodged the next few shots as Speed tried to think of a way to take this guy down.

Soon, they would be out of the mountains and back on flat land. He would have more room to maneuver there. Just then another bullet bounced

off the car's dome. Speed didn't think he could wait that long.

Speed activated the left jacks only. He flipped to his right and landed on the rock wall beside them. He activated the crampons and drove along the near-vertical surface. He slowly climbed up, away from Snake.

Snake put the gun away and tried to do the same. His car jacked into the air and followed Speed to the wall. However, without crampons, Snake couldn't stay vertical. Speed hit the jacks and flipped back to the road. Snake fell back to the road, but he didn't land on all four tires. As an explosion filled Speed's rearview mirror, he could just make out Snake's kwik-save escape cocoon bouncing across the pavement.

Ahead of the pack, Speed, Taejo, and Racer X finished the rest of the rally without incident. With Speed and Racer X just a few feet behind him, Taejo was the first to cross the finish line underneath the checkered flag.

Chapter 23

Speed had only two days to bask in his victory
before Inspector Detector came with bad news.
He explained how Taejo had refused to turn over
evidence against Royalton.

Speed slammed down a wrench in frustration.

"I don't get it," said Sparky. "What happened?"

"The Togokahns played us for chumps," said Pops.
"All they wanted was our help to drive up the stock on
his family's company. Even if there was a file, he had
no intention of turning it over."

"In the end, Royalton got what he wanted," said
the inspector. "He bought Togokahn Motors, albeit at
a higher price than he hoped."

"You mean that whole race was for nothing?"
asked Sparky.

Speed shook his head and leaped into his car.
"Speed, wait," said Pops. But he didn't listen. He
pulled out of the driveway and drove into the night.

Minutes later, he was tearing around the
Thunderhead racetrack. Without the flashing lights,
banners, or crowds, the track was truly his sanctuary.
Driving always helped clear his head. It was as if, at
least for a while anyway, he could pull away from his
problems, leaving them at the starting line.

Speed couldn't believe that everything he'd been

through had been for nothing. He had risked his life to bring down Royalton, to try to clean up racing. And in the end, Royalton got what he wanted. Speed could picture the man sitting back in his spacious office, laughing. Maybe he was right. Maybe that's just the way it was and Speed was a chump to think he could change it. Maybe his brother had died for nothing. There was no way to make a difference.

Movement in the rearview mirror grabbed Speed's attention. For a second he thought it was his brother Rex driving behind him because it matched his moves so perfectly. However, as it drew closer, Speed realized it was the Shooting Star, driven by Racer X.

Suddenly Racer X became the focus of all Speed's frustrations. Wielding his car like a club, Speed took another shot at Racer X. This time, Racer X dodged the blow. This further enraged Speed. He hit the gas and drove straight for the masked racer. He clipped Racer X's rear bumper, sending the yellow car into a spin. It flew off the track and crashed through a barricade. It plowed into the metal stands before stopping.

Speed slammed on the brakes. What had he done? His back wheels burned rubber as he slammed into reverse. He skidded to a stop in front of the hole in the barricades. He leaped from his car and ran toward the crash site.

"X?!" yelled Speed. "Racer X?" As he neared the

car, he saw the masked Racer slumped over the wheel. He stirred slightly. "Racer X?"

Racer X sat up and rubbed the back of his neck. "Wow, kid. You can drive." He laughed. "I haven't been thrown like that in years."

Speed stopped in his tracks and his concern melted away. Now that Racer X wasn't hurt, he felt the anger boil inside again. "What are you doing here?" he asked.

"The inspector told me what happened," Racer X replied. "I came looking for you."

"Why?" asked Speed.

The masked man smiled and climbed out of his car. "I thought you'd take it hard and maybe do something stupid."

Speed snarled. "Why would you care?"

"Because you're a fighter," he replied. "And a friend."

Speed shook his head. "Why don't you just tell me the truth?" He stepped closer. "You're Rex, aren't you?"

"You mean your brother?" asked Racer X.

"You first appeared two years after Rex died," explained Speed. "You drive just like him. You knew I'd be here because this is where he always used to take me. Just tell me the truth."

For a moment, Racer X didn't reply. Then he reached for his mask. Speed's heart skipped a beat as Racer X removed his mask. But the man before

him looked nothing like his brother.

"You're not Rex?" asked Speed.

"No. I'm sorry, Speed. Your brother is dead," said Racer X. He put his mask back on.

Speed hung his head. "I'm sorry."

"Don't be," said Racer X. "I'm sure wherever your brother is, he is immensely proud of you."

"For what?" asked Speed. "Making the same mistakes he did?"

"For trying to make a difference," X explained. "From what I've read, that's all he tried to do."

Tears welled in Speed's eyes. "And what good did it do? He got killed for nothing. Racing hasn't changed and it never will!"

"It doesn't matter if racing ever changes," said X. "What matters is if we let racing change us. Every one of us has to find the reason to do this."

Speed wrung his hands together. "I don't know why I'm even doing it anymore."

"That's obvious," X replied. "At Fuji, you were trying to prove something. At Cristo, you were looking for justice. Neither one is the reason you belong behind a steering wheel."

Speed glared at Racer X. "If you know so much, why don't you tell me why I should keep driving?"

Racer X climbed back into his car. "That's for you to figure out. I just hope when you do, I'm there to see it." Racer X drove down the track and disappeared into the night.

Chapter 24

Speed climbed back into his car. He didn't feel any better. And he didn't have answers to any of his questions. He drove home and went straight to his room. He pulled out a duffle bag and began throwing clothes inside.

"Whatcha doing?" said Spritle.

Speed turned to see Spritle and Chim-Chim standing in the doorway. Speed's jaw clenched as he went back to his packing. "What does it look like?"

"Where are you going?" asked Spritle.

"I don't know," replied Speed. He frantically tossed more clothes into his bag. "I just have to get away from here."

"Can we come with you?" asked Spritle. Chim-Chim nodded his head in agreement. He wanted to go, too.

"No," barked Speed.

"Why not?" asked Spritle.

Suddenly, Speed was struck with déjà vu. He remembered standing exactly where Spritle stood as Rex packed to leave so many years ago. Speed remembered how heartbroken he felt.

"Why can't we come with you?" Spritle asked again.

Speed shook his head and zipped his bag shut.

"You'll understand when it's your turn to leave." He threw the bag over his shoulder and rushed out of the room.

However, as he entered the living room, Pops stood between him and the front door.

"Speed, before you go, I'd like to say a few things," said Pops. "Will you sit with your old man for a minute?"

Speed tensed for an argument. "Don't try to stop me."

Pops shook his head. "I won't. I made a mistake trying to tell you what to do at Cortega. You were right, I was wrong. I won't make that mistake again."

Speed dropped his bag and plopped onto the couch. His father sat in the chair across from him. "I want you to know I acted rashly. I said things I wish I hadn't. Your mother usually protects me from making a fool out of myself. But I was determined to do it this time, and I guess I did a pretty good job at it. I wanted to make sure you understood how sorry I am."

"Thanks," said Speed.

"The truth is, I couldn't have been more proud of you, son," said Pops. "Not because you won, but because you stood up, you weren't afraid, and you did what you thought was right."

"It didn't amount to anything," said Speed. "It was completely meaningless."

"How could it be meaningless?" asked Pops. "I saw my son become a man. I watched him act with courage and integrity and drive the pants off of every driver on the road. This is not meaningless. This is the reason for a father's life."

Speed's lips tightened. His father never told him anything like that before.

"I admit I went to the Casa Cristo because I was afraid," his father explained. "I couldn't lose another one of my boys like that again." He hung his head. "But what I realized in Cortega was that I didn't lose Rex when he crashed, I lost him here. I lost him when he walked out of this house. I let him go without telling him how proud I was of him and how much I loved him."

Pops eyes filled with tears. "You'll never know how much I regret that mistake. But it's enough that I'll never make it again." He stood. "I love you, Speed. I understand that every child leaves home, but I want you to know that door is always open and you can always come back."

Speed got to his feet. "I love you, Pops." He hugged his father. "I'm just so confused right now. I'm locked up in some kind of tailspin and no direction makes sense."

"I know what you mean," said Pops. "When Rex died I didn't even know if I wanted to keep building cars. Then, do you remember that night, when we sat together, watching old Ben Burns and

Stickleton? That night something just clicked."

Speed remembered all too well. In fact, he had just told that story to Royalton. Then the man had promptly crushed his dreams. Speed had never told his father what Royalton had said. Maybe it was about time he did.

Speed stepped back. "That's just it, Pops. That's part of it."

"What?" his father asked.

"That race. The '43 Prix. Burns and Stickleton . . . it was fixed," Speed paced around the room. "Royalton told me the whole story. They've known the winner of every Grand Prix for the past fifty years. It's *always* fixed."

Pops shook his head. "I don't believe that. Royalton's a crook. You can't believe a crook."

"I don't think he was lying, Pops," said Speed.

"The Grand Prix?" asked Pops. "A sham? How could that be?"

Before Speed could explain further, the doorbell rang. He opened the door and was very surprised by whom he saw. "Horuko?"

Taejo's sister gave a polite bow. "Forgive me for intruding, but I had to come before it was too late."

Speed hesitated. He'd been scammed by one Togokahn already. She must have sensed the doubt in his expression.

"This is not a trick, I swear to you," she said. "I am not my brother."

Speed glanced back at Pops. His father shrugged and pointed to the door. "You going to ask the nice lady in?"

Speed opened the door wide and she stepped inside. "My security man believes I am still at the opera, so I only have a moment." She turned to Speed. "I am very sorry for what happened. What my father and brother did was not right, and I am ashamed."

Speed sighed. "It's fine. Just another lesson learned."

"No, *they* are the ones in need of a lesson." She dug through her purse and removed an envelope. "This rightfully belongs to you." She handed it to Speed.

He opened the envelope and pulled out an embossed card. "An invitation to compete in the ninety-first annual Grand Prix?" Speed had given up his dream of ever seeing such an invitation, much less holding one.

"My brother was going to decline, anyway," said Horuko. "But I studied the rules very carefully. As a member of the winning Togokahn Team, if you present this invitation on the day of the race, they *must* allow you to compete."

A grin spread across Pops's face. "What do you think of that, Mr. It's-Always-Fixed?"

Chapter 25

Along with Sparky and Trixie, the entire Racer clan worked tirelessly to rebuild the Mach 6 for the Grand Prix. Even Spritle and Chim-Chim joined in. Royalton had bragged about how his facility could build a car in thirty-six hours. Racer Motors set a personal record when they did it in thirty-two.

They reached the Grand Prix Arena just in time. The enormous venue was already packed. Normally, Speed and his family would have joined the spectators. They would have crammed into seats under the huge dome that encompassed the roller-coaster-like racetrack. This time, Pops, Sparky, and Speed hauled the Mach 6 onto a trailer toward the drivers' entrance.

Unfortunately, Speed's late arrival made arena security question the authenticity of his invitation. They took Speed to the race officials' room. There, the officials passed the invitation back and forth. Speed wondered if they were going to keep him from racing.

Luckily, with impeccable timing, Inspector Detector walked into the room. "Is there a problem here, officer?"

The inspector examined the invitation. Then he and the officials huddled together. Speed couldn't

make out what they said, but things began looking up.

Then Royalton burst into the room. "What madness is going on here?"

"Mr. Royalton, this is a legitimate invitation," said one of the race officials. He handed it to him. "We've verified it."

Royalton examined the card, then narrowed his eyes at Speed. "Where did you get this?"

"I was on the Togokahn Team, remember?" replied Speed. "I won it fair and square."

Royalton threw it to the ground. "This is preposterous! He can't be allowed to race. It's too late!"

"The ruling on this is quite clear," said Inspector Detector. "Try to stop it and you'll be in blatant violation of the WRL charter. You'll leave me no option but to shut down this year's Prix until a full investigation can be completed."

"What?!" yelled Royalton. "Do you have any idea what that would cost? Are you insane?"

The inspector smiled. "Try me."

Royalton glared at Speed. "You'll regret this."

"Doubt it," said Speed.

Once he checked in the Mach 6, Speed went to the racers' locker room. He shared the large space with some of the biggest names in racing: Sonic "Boom-Boom" Renaldi, Prince Kabala, Kellie "Gearbox" Kalinkov, Nitro Venderhoss, and Kakkoii Teppodama.

Some he had even raced against, like Gray Ghost. Others, he had only met, like Royalton's own Jack "Cannonball" Taylor, the two-time Grand Prix Champion. He would be driving Royalton's newest model race car, the GRX, and Speed wondered if Taylor was slated to win this race. That's probably why Royalton was so upset about Speed entering. Speed Racer was a wild card. No one could tell him what to do.

Speed felt awkward as he suited up. All the other racers seemed to be staring at him. He didn't know why, but it felt like some of them wanted to take a swing at him before the race even began. He felt like a gazelle that suddenly found himself among a pack of lions.

As Speed turned back to his locker, there was a tap on his shoulder. "Hey, kid," said a driver.

Speed jumped with a start. He turned to see . . . Gray Ghost.

The tall driver extended a hand. "Just wanted to wish you luck." When Speed shook his hand, the Ghost pulled him close. "There's a million dollar bounty on your head," he whispered.

"A million dollars," Speed repeated. He wasn't surprised at all. It seemed like the kind of dirty move Royalton would make. "Maybe I should take myself out," Speed said.

"Watch yourself," warned Gray Ghost. "You're ruffling some pretty major feathers out there."

"Why aren't *you* after the bounty?" asked Speed.

The man smiled. "Our little dance at Fuji . . . that's how it should always be." He gave Speed a nod and walked away.

It felt good to be respected by a fellow driver. It even took away some of the apprehension he felt about having a bounty on his head. Unfortunately, his hopes sank as he dug through his duffle bag. He searched the outside pockets, the inside pockets, the very bottom. Nothing. His lucky red socks were nowhere to be found.

"Speed Racer?" came a voice behind him. "I'm quite a fan of yours."

He didn't have time for this. He spun around to see a tall man in an expensive suit. It took a second for Speed to realize that the man was Racer X without the mask.

"Oh, hi," said Speed.

Racer X smiled. "I'm very glad to see you here." Then his smile faded. "Is something wrong?"

Speed ran a hand across the back of his neck. "I just . . . I have this thing . . . ," said Speed. "It's stupid, I know. Just a superstition . . ."

"Can I help?" asked the unmasked racer.

"I don't think . . ." Then Speed noticed the racer's suit. The man wore a red tie with a matching red handkerchief. He wondered what else matched.

Chapter 26

Wearing Racer X's red socks, Speed pulled the Mach 6 out onto the track. He lined up behind the rest of the racers. Since he didn't qualify for the Grand Prix and was there by special invitation only, Speed had to take the last starting position.

The racetrack venue was the biggest in which he had ever raced. The track twisted and spiraled right up to the top of the domed coliseum. A giant video monitor hovered above the track. Speed was shocked to see his face on the huge screen. He quickly turned his attention back to the Mach 6. Even though the coliseum was huge, his car's cockpit was the same size as always.

The thunder of revving engines filled the air as the drivers warmed up their cars. Speed started the Mach 6, and it vibrated every part of his body. It sounded and felt better than ever.

He concentrated on that sound as the countdown began. By the time the count was at zero, he was at one with the Mach 6.

Speed hit the gas and swerved past three cars. Starting last, he would have to work hard to cover as much track as possible.

He slammed on the brakes as he approached a car directly ahead. The car was driving much too

slowly. Speed wondered if the driver had engine trouble as he gripped the wheel. He was about to pass, when another car appeared to his left. Then one more was on his right. He was completely blocked in. It hadn't taken long for the other drivers to make their move.

Another car was closing in on Speed from behind. It was flying toward him at incredible speed. Speed activated only the right jump jacks just in time. He flipped to his left, over one of the cars and back onto the track. He peeled away just as the car that was coming from behind him plowed into the other cars that had tried to box him in. They erupted in a giant fireball.

Speed had to fight for his life the entire first lap of the track. Every car he tried to pass attacked with a brutality he'd never seen before. His million-dollar bounty certainly meant more than winning to many of the other drivers. They came at him at every jump, through the high-walled turn, and the pylon-dotted slalom.

"This is crazy," commented Sparky through the headset.

Luckily, their aggressiveness worked in Speed's favor. He used their blind tenacity to lure them into crashing into one another. Others were driving so aggressively that they took turns so fast that they flew off the raised track and crashed to the ground below. No matter how it played out, Speed Racer

battled his way up from last place. The track behind him was littered with fire, debris, and bouncing kwik-save cocoons.

On the next lap, Speed caught up to the small pack of lead cars. While Gray Ghost battled the jewel-encrusted car of Prince Kabala, Speed passed them, heading for the leader—Cannonball Taylor. Soon he was bumper-to-bumper with Royalton's star driver.

"Okay, Mr. Two-Time Grand Prix, future Hall of Famer," said Speed. "Teach me something."

Speed jerked the wheel and hit the gas. Soon he drove alongside the purple car. Cannonball came at him with a clumsy swerve. Speed easily dodged it as they drifted through a tight turn.

"Come on!" said Speed. "Is that it?"

The purple car fenced with the Mach 6 but Speed easily parried every attack. He was on top of his game. He was at one with his race car and no one could take him down. He decided to take Cannonball down on the next straightaway.

"Lesson's over," said Speed. He jerked the wheel left, shoving Cannonball against the guardrail. "See you at the finish line."

Suddenly, he felt a familiar *THUD* through the floorboard. "No!" he shouted.

"What is it?" asked Sparky.

"Spear hook!" Speed replied. He tried to pull away from Cannonball but he was stuck to him like

glue. "He's got me!" Speed shouted.

Speed punched the gas and jerked the wheel. He tried to break free, but it was no good. At most, he was only able to steer both cars together. Since Cannonball fought to stay attached, it felt as if he were piloting an aircraft carrier instead of a race car.

Cars zipped around them as they swerved back and forth across the track. Sparks flew from the Mach 6 as Cannonball scraped Speed against the guardrail. The steering wheel trembled in Speed's hands as he fought back. He hit the gas, shoving the purple car against the guardrail on the left. Sparks flew as it scraped against the metal.

Even though cars were passing them, they still zipped down the track at a tremendous speed. With hardly any control, it was only a matter of time before their predicament wrecked them both.

Speed looked up to see the slalom course ahead. The forest of concrete pylons was growing fast. If he didn't do something soon, Taylor would ram the Mach 6 into one of the pylons.

At the last second, Speed activated the right set of jump jacks. The force of the jacks caused both cars to flip to the side. They zipped through the pylons on one set of Taylor's wheels. Speed glanced up at the giant video screen to see an image of their undercarriages. The spear hook was splayed across the screen for all to see. Whether

or not Speed got out of this mess, everyone would know that Cannonball Taylor was cheating. And since Royalton Industries built his car and all its modifications, Royalton would be held responsible as well.

With all four tires off the road, the Mach 6 caught air and swiveled. As Taylor's car slammed back to the ground, Speed's car smashed across the top of him. The spear hook was knocked free and both cars spun across the track. The purple car skidded to a stop against the guardrail.

Speed shifted to first and hit the gas. Nothing happened. The Mach 6 was dead.

"No, no, no, no!" shouted Speed. "Don't do this!" He turned the ignition key, but nothing happened. The Mach 6 refused to start.

Up in his Grand Prix Luxury Box, Racer X watched Speed struggle to restart the Mach 6. "Careful," Racer X said quietly. "Listen to it, don't kill the starter."

Back on the track, Speed thought back to what his brother taught him. Rex told him to always listen to his car. Speed closed his eyes and cleared his mind of all mechanical fixes. *What did the Mach 6 want? How would it start?* "What do you need?" he whispered.

Speed took a deep breath. He tuned out the roaring engines and the cheering crowd. It was just him and the Mach 6.

Suddenly, it hit him. He shoved it into second gear and slammed down the accelerator. He turned the starter and the engine roared to life. He left off the clutch and peeled out. The sound of his screeching tires was quickly drowned out by the cheers of the entire coliseum.

Speed drove like he was alone on the track. He was half a lap away from the leaders of the race and he had to make up time. He flew by other cars as if they were standing still. Those who tried to grapple with him didn't have a prayer.

The lead cars were in sight when Speed hit the spiral turn. Speed climbed the track faster than he would have thought possible. It was as if a crowbar couldn't pry his tires from the track. He clenched his teeth as the g-force tried to rip him from the cockpit.

Foot by foot, inch by inch, he gained on the last two cars, one of which was Gray Ghost. Speed nearly drove the gas pedal through the floorboard as he neared the big drop. He sailed into the air, soaring high above the track. When he touched down, he was right behind Gray Ghost.

They pulled into the final straightaway. The gray car feigned left then right, not letting Speed get a shot. Speed then mimicked the driver. He used the same trick Gray Ghost used on everyone else.

"Now you see me, now you don't," said Speed. He swerved back and forth and Gray Ghost didn't know

where Speed was coming from. Gray Ghost began making mistakes, overcompensating.

As they neared the finish line, Speed made his move. He tore up the left side of Gray Ghost. The gray car swung at him, trying to bat him away. Speed hit the jacks and flew into the air. Gray Ghost spun out and slammed into the retaining wall. Speed zoomed through the cloud of smoke and fire, and crossing into history, he saw the black-and-white checkered flag wave in front of him.

Racer X and Inspector Detector observed the race from Racer X's private booth. Both were beaming with pride and satisfaction over Speed's victory.

"He did it," said Inspector Detector.

Racer X chuckled and shook his head. "Yes, he did."

"This could change everything, you know," said the inspector.

"It already has," said Racer X.

In the Grand Prix penthouse, E.P. Arnold Royalton, Esquire, sat slumped in a thick leather chair. He stared in disbelief at the finish line. His booth was once full of important guests. Now he was the only one there. Racer X suspected that that was going to be the new theme of Royalton's life. With the loss of his prized racer and the fact that everyone knew he was a cheater, the racing community would have nothing to do with him. His

company's stock would plummet. He would probably file for bankruptcy within the week. The entire CIB had tried, but couldn't manage to take him down. But it looked as if Speed Racer did it all by himself. Racer X was very proud of young Speed.

"My men are bringing the family down to the finish line," said the inspector. "Do you want to go with them?"

Racer X shook his head. "No."

The inspector shrugged his shoulders and headed for the door. Before leaving, he stopped and turned back to Racer X. "Can I ask you a question? Do you ever think you made a mistake?" he asked. "Hiding the truth from them?"

Racer X gazed out over the track. As his eyes focused on the smoldering debris of the crashed race cars, he thought back to the Maltese Ice Caves. It had been ten years since he'd faked his own death. Soon after, the finest CIB surgeons had changed his face. He thought back to some of his previous undercover missions. Rex Racer couldn't have gone on those missions. But Racer X could.

"If I did make a mistake," said Rex Racer. "Then it's one I have to live with."

At the victory lane, Speed handed Sparky one of the bottles of ice-cold milk. They tapped the jugs together before taking deep drinks. To Speed, milk had never tasted so good.

It seemed as if the entire coliseum had hopped

the barriers and stormed onto the track. The crowd chanted Speed's name as they encircled the Mach 6. Even some of the other drivers stood among them, applauding Speed. Out front was Gray Ghost himself. He gave Speed a knowing nod.

A gap appeared in the crowd as CIB men escorted the Racer family through.

"Speed!" yelled Trixie, running ahead of them. Speed sprung from the car and ran to her. He swooped her into his arms and kissed her in front of the flashing cameras. The two of them were even projected onto the giant screen above.

Spritle covered Chim-Chim's eyes. "Danger. May cause cooties." The rest of his family swooped in and embraced him.

A reporter pushed his way out of the surrounding crowd. He held out a microphone. "How did you do it, Speed?" he asked. "What's your secret?"

"A driver is only as good as his car," Speed replied. "His car . . . and his support team." Speed glanced around at the smiling faces of his friends and family. He had the best team in the world.

SPEED RACER
THE VIDEOGAME

RACING INTO STORES MAY 2008
SEE THE MOVIE ONLY IN THEATERS!

RATING PENDING
RP
CONTENT RATED BY
ESRB

Visit www.esrb.org
for updated rating
information.

WB GAMES™

Wii™

NINTENDO DS